# CHRISTMAS AT CARLY'S CUPCAKES

CAN CHRISTMAS WISHES COME TRUE …
EVENTUALLY?

JESSICA REDLAND

Boldwood

First published in Great Britain in 2020 by Boldwood Books Ltd.

A CIP catalogue record for this book is available from the British Library.

Paperback ISBN 978-1-80048-344-6

Large Print ISBN 978-1-80048-343-9

Ebook ISBN 978-1-80048-000-1

Kindle ISBN 978-1-80048-001-8

Audio CD ISBN 978-1-80048-338-5

MP3 CD ISBN 978-1-80048-339-2

Digital audio download ISBN 978-1-80048-341-5

Boldwood Books Ltd
23 Bowerdean Street
London SW6 3TN
www.boldwoodbooks.com

*At the heart of this story is the relationship between two sisters, Carly and Bethany. It would therefore be logical to dedicate this book to my sister ... but I don't have one. This is therefore dedicated to the next best thing, my sisters-in-law: Clare, Linda, Sue and Vanessa. Hugs to you all xx*

# 1

'Argh! Carly! Help!'

Heart racing at the anguished cry, I dropped my bookings diary on the counter and dashed into the workshop at the back of my shop. 'What's wrong?'

My younger sister looked up from the table. 'It's awful. I've killed Santa.'

I looked into her mournful blue eyes and couldn't help laughing.

'It's not funny,' Bethany protested. 'I've killed a snowman and a reindeer too.' She folded her arms and pouted like a petulant child. She looked and sounded more like she was ten than twenty-three. 'I'm so rubbish at this. I'm rubbish at everything I do.'

I moved round to survey her handiwork. 'Oh,' I said, unable to keep the disappointment out of my voice.

'I did warn you,' she said defensively.

'Erm... well, as I always say, it takes patience and practice.' I could hear the lack of conviction in my words.

Bethany shook her head, picked up the Santa cupcake, peeled off the messy wrapper and took a large bite. 'I don't have any patience, as you well know,' she mumbled through a mouthful of sponge. 'And I've been practising for months now. I'm getting worse instead of better, aren't I?'

I'd have loved to give her some reassurance but she was right. After four months of working in my shop – Carly's Cupcakes in the North Yorkshire seaside town of Whitsborough Bay – Bethany had perfected the ability to bake beautiful, light sponge cakes but she had zero talent when it came to decorating them. She hadn't even mastered a basic buttercream swirl and her iced figures were unidentifiable. If her task was simply to attach one of my figures to a cake I'd prepared, she somehow managed to squash the figure, flatten the swirl and smear buttercream all over the wrapper and the table.

Today's attempts were so squashed and out-of-shape that they resembled roadkill – not exactly the jolly festive vibe I was aiming for.

'I'm a liability,' Bethany wailed, wiping buttercream off her chin. She released her long blonde highlighted hair from its ponytail and shook it out as she stepped away from the table. 'I told you that you shouldn't employ me.'

'You are *not* a liability.' I handed Bethany a damp cloth so she could wipe her sticky fingers. 'It's just going to take more patience and practice than we might have hoped.'

'There you go again. Patience and practice. How long does it take?' She narrowed her eyes at me. 'I bet you could do everything perfectly on your first attempt, couldn't you?'

I grimaced. Maybe not *first* attempt, but I'd never found any of the cake decorating techniques a challenge. From the moment I picked up a piping bag and created my first swirl, I knew I'd found my talent.

'I knew it!' Bethany cried. 'You're a success at whatever you do whereas I fail at everything.'

I raised my eyebrows at her. 'Ooh, I think someone's being a little overly dramatic, aren't they?' Taking the cloth from her, I wiped the table.

She folded her arms across her chest. 'Name one thing I've done better than you,' she challenged.

'Easy. What are you doing on 22nd December?'

She shrugged. 'Getting married.'

'Exactly.' I stepped into the small kitchen next to the workshop and rinsed the cloth. 'I might be sorted with my career but my love life's a disaster,' I called to her. 'You'll find a job that suits you eventually but you know there's a role here for as long as you want it.' I wiped my hands and stepped back into the workshop. 'You're brilliant with customers and you can't deny that. And you know I love you being here. It's my fault for putting too much pressure on you. Maybe you should stick to baking cakes and serving in the shop for now.'

Bethany picked up another destroyed cupcake, unwrapped it, and took a bite. I raised my eyebrows at her.

'What? It's not like you'd have been able to sell them. They're beyond saving.' She scrunched up the wrapper and tossed it towards the bin but it bounced off the side and landed in the middle of the floor.

'Are you going to leave that there?' I asked, keeping my tone light even though leaving a mess like that was a pet peeve of mine and Bethany knew it. She often accused me of being too health and safety conscious but that was because she was new to catering and simply couldn't see the risks. I let my sister get away with a lot but I drew the line at a messy workplace.

With an exaggerated sigh, Bethany picked up the wrapper, placed it deliberately in the bin and sat back down at the table. 'When you said you needed someone to help in the shop, you were after someone you could train to take the pressure off you, not someone who would create you twice as much work.'

'It's not that bad.'

'It is! My decorating skills are worse than a toddler's and I make more of a mess than they would.' She swept her arm across the table.

I didn't mean to do it but my eyes automatically flicked towards the wall where I'd already spotted several splats of red and green buttercream as well as some icing trails.

Bethany must have followed my eye line. 'No! How have I managed to decorate the wall too?'

I moved towards the wall but she grabbed the cloth from my hands. 'It's my mess,' she muttered. 'I'll sort it out.'

The doorbell tinkled indicating the arrival of a customer. Trying not to cringe as Bethany managed to smear the red buttercream across my pristine white paintwork instead of wiping it off, I headed through the archway into the shop.

'Sorry to have kept you,' I said to the customer. 'How can I help?'

She smiled. 'My name's Jen. Jen Alderson. I got a text to say the birthday cake I'd ordered was ready.'

'Ah, yes, it's all done.'

I turned and carefully lifted the sturdy cake box off a shelving unit behind me. Placing it on the counter, I lifted the lid and deftly unhooked the side flaps, revealing a woodland-themed birthday cake. A large, round tree stump with a fox on top of it was surrounded by cupcakes decorated like toadstools on which a rabbit, owl, badger and squirrel were seated. A number four sign hung on the front of the tree stump and letters stating, 'Happy 4th Birthday Freddie' were secured to the green icing base. I'd had such fun creating it but, as always, experienced a brief moment of nervous tension that it wouldn't meet the customer's expectations.

She'd been quite vague about what she wanted and I feared that, one day, a customer's vision and my interpretation of it would be a disastrous miss-match.

Jen gasped. 'Oh my goodness, Freddie's going to love that. Thank you so much. It's even better than I imagined. So much detail.'

I smiled, the tension leaving my shoulders. Nailed it. 'Thank you. I'm glad you like it.'

'I love it. Am I too late to order a Christmas cake?'

'I'm fully booked for anything complex but I'm still taking orders for simpler designs. Do you know what you'd like?'

She chatted through some ideas and showed me some designs she'd saved to her phone but it was hard to concentrate with Bethany clattering about in the workshop. What on earth was she doing? I hoped she wasn't rearranging the kitchen again. Last time she'd decided to be 'helpful' like that, I hadn't been able to find anything.

Jen placed an order for a chocolate cake shaped like a reindeer's head with chocolate antlers, then thanked me again and left with the woodland birthday cake.

There was a squeal and another clatter from the workshop. I took a deep breath before going to investigate.

As soon as I stepped through the archway, I felt my body deflate as I took in the carnage.

'Oh my goodness! Bethany!' I couldn't keep the despair out of my voice.

'It wasn't my fault.' Her shoulders sank. 'Actually, it was. I thought I'd try again and do what you said – patience and practice – but the piping bag exploded. I'm sorry, Carly. I tried to clear it up but I think I made it worse.'

I closed my eyes for a moment in the desperate hope that, when I opened them, I'd discover I'd been hallucinating and Bethany hadn't really managed to cover the table, walls and floor in globs of red butter icing. Or – far worse – the sixty cupcakes I'd already decorated for tomorrow night's Christmas lights switch-on.

'You're mad at me, aren't you?' Bethany whined.

I opened my eyes. Damn. No hallucination. The thought of all the re-work needed filled me with panic and I blinked back tears. I fought to keep my voice light and steady, anxious that Bethany wouldn't see how bad this was. 'I'm not mad.'

'Yes you are.' Her voice wobbled.

'Okay, I am a bit, but these things happen. It's not the end of the world.' Although it felt pretty close at that moment, knowing how much other work I had to do. The cupcakes could potentially have been salvageable but it looked like she'd already attempted that and they now resembled the roadkill calamities she'd created herself.

'Why are some on them on the floor?'

She cringed as she glanced down at the dozen or so cakes splatted near her feet, all buttercream side down. 'I knocked a tray over when I was trying to clean the wall. I'm so sorry. Should I start baking some new ones?'

What I really wanted was for Bethany to leave the premises so I could start over in safety.

'Hopefully Joshua's parents will understand if I'm late again,' she added, distinct uncertainty in her voice.

She was having dinner with Margaret and Damian, her future in-laws, with whom she had a somewhat shaky relationship. They'd made it clear that they thought Joshua and Bethany were too young to get married and had often passed comment on Bethany's seeming inability to hold down a steady job. I knew they made her nervous and that it broke her heart that they hadn't welcomed her into their family with the same love and enthusiasm our parents had shown towards Joshua. I didn't want to add any fuel to the fire by making her late and it was the perfect excuse for me to start over on the cakes without her.

I gave her a reassuring smile. 'Tell you what, as it's nearly closing time, why don't you head off and get yourself ready and I'll finish off here?'

'But the mess...'

'I'll sort it. See you tomorrow?'

'If you're sure it's okay to go?'

*I couldn't be surer.* 'Definitely. Off you go and get that seating plan sorted. Sit me next to someone nice.'

Bethany removed her apron and flashed me a grateful smile. 'Thank you. You're a saint.'

'I know,' I muttered under my breath as she grabbed her bag and coat from the hooks on the wall. *Only a saint would give you this many chances.*

## 2

As soon as the door closed, I released a sigh of relief. Peace and quiet was restored. I shook my head at the carnage once more then grabbed the bin and swept the cupcakes into it, cringing at the waste. I filled a bowl with hot, soapy water and started scrubbing.

Although I'd never admit it to her, Bethany was right about being a liability but what could I do? I couldn't sack my own sister, especially not after the incident in her previous job. She'd been so excited when she started the role at Sandy Shores Nursery last year. The first nine months went brilliantly and she radiated with happiness. Mum, Dad and I were convinced she'd finally found her vocation in life after a few false starts in hairdressing, dog-grooming and lifeguarding. The children loved her, she got on well with the other staff, she sped through her first qualification with ease and her manager was considering fast-tracking her to the next level.

Then it happened. An estranged father with a grudge, a drugs problem, and a knife turned up at home time and tried to grab his three-year-old son.

When Mum phoned me in tears to say they were on their way to Whitsborough Bay General Hospital because Bethany had been stabbed, I feared the worst. By the time I arrived at the hospital, I'd been bordering on hysteria. I found Joshua and my parents in the waiting room, pacing up and down, anxious for the verdict. Thankfully it was a positive one. The knife had missed any vital organs and arteries and, despite losing a lot of blood, medical staff assured us there was no reason Bethany wouldn't make a full recovery.

I'd always felt fiercely protective towards my younger sister. At eight years her senior, it had been an instinctive older sibling thing but she was one of those accident-prone kids so I worried about her constantly and our parents were exactly the same. We never made a fuss when Bethany announced each new career choice, reassuring her it was more important to be happy and even encouraging her to leave if she wasn't feeling satisfied. Too late, we collectively realised we should have challenged her more. We should have explained that most jobs included undesirable tasks and bad days. We should have given her coping mechanisms so she could build up her resilience. Hindsight was a great thing.

After the stabbing, the desire to protect her was stronger than ever. I was certain that, if my parents could have put her in a bubble and moved her back home, they would have. I certainly wanted to. She was in good hands with Joshua, though. He couldn't have been more perfect for Bethany. Even though they were the same age, he was thoughtful and mature beyond his years, which provided the perfect balance and grounded my sister. They'd met two years ago when she was a lifeguard. A young boy badly misjudged a dive into the pool and landed on top of Joshua, knocking him unconscious. Bethany had pulled Joshua from the water and resuscitated him. He'd waited for her after work a few days later with a bouquet of flowers and a dinner invitation. They'd moved in together after only six months but it didn't feel hasty. Anyone seeing them together could see how deeply they loved each other.

Physically, Bethany did heal but the emotional scars ran deeper.

Mum, Dad, Joshua and I were all convinced it was too early but Bethany insisted she was ready to return to the nursery as soon as she was signed off as fit for work. It was the first time she'd shown so much passion for a job and the first time she'd shown such determination so we had no choice but to stand back and hope she was as ready as she claimed.

She returned to work with a smile on her face, laughing at how worried we all were, full of reassurances that she'd be fine. By late morning, her manager found her curled up in a ball on the floor of the staff toilets, sobbing uncontrollably.

Joshua took more leave from work while Bethany further convalesced but when he couldn't take any more time off, he expressed concern about leaving her alone. She claimed she didn't need a 'babysitter' but she wasn't fooling any of us. Her sparkle had gone. Her zest for life had gone. Pale-faced and jumpy, my fun-loving sister had gone.

I suggested she keep me company at the shop and was both surprised and relieved when she agreed, although she spent the first fortnight in my flat above the shop rather than with me. She napped, watched TV or flicked through magazines, only wandering down the internal stairs occasionally to say hello and make me a drink.

The haunted expression on her face – hollow cheeks, wide eyes – filled me with dread and I worried we'd lost her. I suggested she go back to her doctor but she was adamant that all she needed was time. I didn't push further in case my nagging stopped her coming to the shop each day. Mum, Dad and Joshua all mooted the idea of professional help but the suggestion made her angry or tearful so they backed down too. We all hoped she was right about just needing time.

During the third week at mine, she stayed downstairs with me for a little longer each day. By the fourth week, she spent some full days with me and the change in her during that fortnight filled me with hope. She chatted, made jokes and even served a few customers when I was in the middle of trickier tasks.

By week five, Bethany was downstairs with me full-time every day and her fun, bubbly personality seemed to be back. She'd always had a gift for accents and had me in stitches as she impersonated some of the demanding or quirky customers she'd encountered in her various jobs. She told amusing stories of naughty dogs and their lookalike customers from her grooming days and tales of calling time on amorous couples in the pool when she was a lifeguard.

During quiet moments, we'd stand by the shop windows looking out over Castle Street and she'd make up stories about the people passing, enacting hilarious conversations she imagined them having, until tears ran down my cheeks and I had a stitch from laughing so much.

After six weeks, she announced that she was ready to return to her role at Sandy Shores Nursery. She looked ready. She acted ready. She didn't make it past the gates.

She sat beside me in the workshop later that day, her pale face streaked with tears.

'What will I do now?' she asked me. 'I loved that job but it's obvious I'm never going to be able to go back.'

My need to keep her safe and protected kicked in. 'Why don't you work for me?'

Her eyes lit up for a moment, then quickly clouded. 'Doing what? It's not busy enough to have someone in the shop full-time and I've already proved useless when it comes to icing cakes.' She'd made a few attempts at icing over the past fortnight and they hadn't gone well.

'Yes, but that's because I haven't trained you properly. You were just playing. With a bit of practice and patience, I could get you up to speed. And you know I was thinking about taking someone on.'

She pondered for a moment. 'I need to talk to Joshua. Can I let you know tomorrow?'

'Of course. And if you do accept the job but you don't like it, you feel ready to apply for a job at another nursery, or you want to try out a new career, then you just need to say. I'm not going to trap you here forever.'

She gave me a weak smile. 'It has to work both ways. If you think I'm rubbish, you have to sack me.'

'You won't be rubbish.'

'Carly!'

'Okay. I promise to dismiss you if you're rubbish. But you won't be. And it'll be fun.' I gave her a big smile. 'Talk it over with Joshua. I won't be offended if you say no but I'd love it if you say yes. It's been a quiet four years working on my own and it's been lovely having company again.'

And it really had been. I'd studied catering at college and had secured a full-time apprenticeship afterwards with Mrs Armstrong, the owner of the imaginatively named The Cake Shop on the outskirts of Whitsborough Bay's town centre, so I'd spent the first nine years of my working life with constant company. Then Mrs Armstrong dropped the bombshell that the estate agent next door wanted to expand into our premises and had made her an offer too good to refuse.

It wasn't long after I'd opened Carly's Cupcakes that I started craving company. I loved the interaction with customers but it was intermittent and I really missed having colleagues to chat to or run ideas by. With the business in its infancy, I couldn't risk employing anyone until I was certain I could earn enough to sustain another salary. At the start of this year, after good year-on-year growth, I'd made the decision to recruit in the summer so I genuinely did have a vacancy for Bethany.

To my delight and relief, she accepted the job. Our parents and Joshua all thought it was a brilliant idea, separately admitting to me that they were grateful I'd be able to keep an eye on her. It really had been great at first. We'd chatted and sang our way through each day and we'd laughed at her many disasters. But now, looking at the carnage in the workshop, it wasn't funny anymore. December was my busiest time of the year and my sister was costing me time and money. Despite my promise to dismiss her if she was 'rubbish', I couldn't let her go, but there was no way we could continue like this. I was going to need to re-think her role. So much for the little fantasy I'd had about her being my apprentice and us working side by side to create beautiful cakes.

My phone rang, making me jump. Bethany.

'What did you forget?' I asked.

'Nothing! I just wanted to ask you something about the seating plan. A few of Joshua's school friends are still single so I wondered if—'

'Don't you dare! They'll all be eight years younger than me.'

'So?'

I shuddered. 'It's icky.'

'How's it icky?'

'When I had my first *proper* relationship,' I massively empha-sised the word to make sure my meaning was clear, 'you, Joshua, and his friends were in your final year of primary school. Need I say more?'

'Ew! That *is* icky!'

'Exactly. So don't even *think* about setting me up.'

'Okay. I promise. You've made your point disgustingly and effec-tively. See you tomorrow.'

'Will do. Bye.'

I hung up, shuddering again. The ickiness wasn't the only reason for me avoiding a setup. The main reason was that I didn't want to meet someone. The deed was already done. I was already truly, madly, deeply in love and, unfortunately, he didn't feel the same way.

## 3

'Did you get the seating plan finalised?' I called from the workshop when Bethany arrived at the shop shortly before ten the following morning.

'Yes, but it took ages,' she called back. 'I knew Joshua had a big family but I had no idea it was so complicated. We've got aunties not speaking to uncles, a homophobic grandma and a gay grandson, cousins at war and goodness knows what else. When Margaret suggested we might need some assistance, I thought she was interfering as usual, but we seriously needed help. I think we've *finally* got a version that will avoid the outbreak of World War III.'

'Family politics, eh? Sounds fun. And I'm sat next to...?'

She headed through to the workshop, unwinding her scarf. 'I can't remember. Sorry. I think I might have put you next to Paige.'

My stomach sank and I tried to keep the edge from my tone. 'Your bridesmaid, Paige?' I was one of seven bridesmaids, alongside Bethany's four best friends and a couple of Joshua's young nieces. I'd never warmed to Paige. She'd been friends with Bethany since primary school so she'd spent loads of time at our house when Bethany was growing up. I'd found her to be loud and bossy and, from what I'd seen recently, those qualities hadn't diminished in adulthood. I'd never breathed a word to Bethany, though, so I'd just have to hope that the person sat on the other side of me at the wedding was more my cup of tea.

Bethany shrugged off her coat and hung it up. 'I think so. Or is she on the friends table? I honestly can't remember. There were so many versions. I promise it's not one of Joshua's single friends, though, and it's not the auntie with the flatulence problem.'

'I'm pleased to hear it.'

The other adult bridesmaids – Amanda, Robyn, and Leyla – were friends of Bethany's from senior school. I'd met them on a few occasions when I'd still been living at home, but had never exchanged more conversation than a passing 'hello'. The day we choose the bridesmaid dresses and then the hen do in November had been the first real opportunities to get to know them. Although they were very giggly and a bit immature, I'd found them to be very friendly and welcoming. By contrast, despite having known her for years, I'd found Paige to be quite cold; almost hostile. I'd wondered whether she resented me being chief bridesmaid after she'd repeatedly pointed out that she'd known Bethany the longest. I hadn't been petty enough to point out that I actually held that accolade.

When we were looking at bridesmaid dresses, Paige had been an absolute pain. A voluptuous size sixteen, she was critical of every style suggested, putting herself down for being larger than the others. They rallied round her, assuring her that she was beautiful with an amazing figure, which I had to agree with. With dimples, an English Rose perfect complexion, and black, glossy curls, Paige was striking but I was certain that she knew it too. Her self-deprecating approach came across to me as pure attention-seeking.

Joshua's family were Scottish and Bethany had chosen a bluey-grey colour to match their family kilt but, with sizes ranging from eight to sixteen, finding a style to suit everyone presented a challenge. Mum suggested we all have the same full-length tulle-covered skirt but a different bodice to suit each bridesmaid's body shape. Even Paige couldn't disagree with that.

I started to notice that Paige didn't just direct jibes at herself; she made constant little digs at the others. They were subtle, but they were definitely there, whether it was about Leyla's petite size eight frame, the gap between Amanda's front teeth, Robyn's auburn hair or Bethany being a 'princess'. Mum clearly noticed it too and we exchanged looks several times but neither of us voiced our concerns because none of the others seemed fazed by Paige's comments. We were probably being overly protective as usual.

I was determined to give Paige the benefit of the doubt and try to enjoy her company at Bethany's hen do but, by the time we'd finished our meal, I'd taken a strong dislike to her. Loud and lairy with a few drinks inside her, the subtle put-downs became less subtle and more abusive. I lost count of the amount of times she called Bethany 'ditzy', 'clumsy' or 'forgetful'. The strange thing was, my sister and her other friends genuinely didn't seem to notice, so I had to conclude that it was my issue, not Paige's.

'Cuppa?' Bethany asked, bringing my focus back to the present.

'Yes, please.'

She made her way into the kitchen. 'Oh my God! You finished them.'

I turned to face her. 'I baked fresh ones last night then came down early this morning to decorate them.'

'How early?'

'About five o'clock.'

'Five?' Bethany leaned against the kitchen doorway; eyes wide. 'I'm so sorry.'

'It's done. Forget about it,' I said gently. Then I smiled and adopted a begging tone. 'Just please promise me you won't go anywhere near the new batch, especially not with a loaded piping bag.'

She nodded solemnly. 'I won't. I promise to stay on the shop side all day.'

Sighing, Bethany backed into the kitchen and filled the kettle. She couldn't ice cakes but she did have her uses – my sister could make the perfect cup of tea.

'So what happens at this Christmas lights switch-on thingy?' Bethany asked, handing me a mug of tea five minutes later. 'Does everyone bring food?'

I shook my head. 'No. Just me, and Tara provides hot drinks for everyone.' My friend, Tara, owned The Chocolate Pot, the café next door to us. She'd opened up roughly a decade before me and had been really generous with her advice and help over the years.

'And they don't pay for it?' Bethany asked.

'No.'

She frowned. 'Then why is it down to you two? It must cost you both a fortune.'

I shook my head. 'I only make basic cupcakes so the cost isn't huge. It usually leads to them buying a batch of cupcakes at some point before Christmas and reminds them to use me for their next occasion cake so it's win-win all round.'

'That's okay, then.' She patted my arm. 'Wouldn't like to think anyone was taking advantage of my sister's kindness.'

I had to cover my mouth with my mug so she couldn't see me smiling at the irony of her comment. Tara had repeatedly suggested that Bethany was taking advantage of my kindness and had definitely outstayed her welcome, reminding me of Bethany's open invitation to dismiss her if she was 'rubbish'. I'd certainly been tempted after yesterday's fiasco but a late night and an early morning had put me back on track and it didn't seem such a crisis anymore. It wasn't the first time and certainly wouldn't be the last time I'd put in hours like that. I'd pulled a few all-nighters over the years to keep on top of orders and none of those could be blamed on my sister. Besides, what would she do if she didn't work with me? I preferred having her where I knew she was safe.

Bethany wandered over to the window and looked up and down Castle Street which was already bustling with Christmas shoppers clutching armloads of bags. 'Will there be lots of people there tonight?' I could hear the tension in her voice. Six months on from the stabbing and she was still wary about crowds of strangers.

'Nothing like the numbers at the big tree. Maybe fifty or sixty people but it's only the traders and their families. It's a lovely atmosphere and perfect for getting into the Christmas spirit.'

Every year on the first Saturday in December, the town's Christmas lights were switched on. An enormous crowd always gathered round the giant Christmas tree outside the shopping centre near the top of town. DJs from Bay Radio would build the revellers into an excited frenzy, culminating in a countdown. A local celebrity – typically a Z-list one who'd auditioned for a reality TV show five years ago – would press the button to light the tree from bottom to top. As soon as the star lit up, the rest of the lights up and down the pedestrianised precinct would illuminate in waves, heralding the arrival of Christmas in Whitsborough Bay.

Castle Street – a side street a little way down the pedestrianised precinct – had white lights tightly strung in a zigzag from the buildings at one side of the cobbled street to the other, creating a stunning blanket of stars between the shops and cafés. Like the rest of the town's lights, they lit up a section at a time, until they reached the Christmas tree in Castle Park – a small park over the road at the end of the street. And it was there that the traders had gathered for the past decade for a private celebration, catching up over a cup of tea, coffee or hot chocolate from The Chocolate Pot.

Shortly before I opened the shop in October four years ago, I'd traipsed up and down Castle Street armed with a pocketful of business cards. I'd introduced myself to each of the traders and handed over a card, asking them to think of me for birthdays, weddings, anniversaries or any other special occasion. Everyone had been friendly, welcoming me to the street and wishing me luck, but a few jokingly asked where their free sample was. I kicked myself for a blindingly obvious missed business opportunity. So when Tara, who'd taken me under her wing, invited me to the traders' Christmas lights switchon that first year and mentioned that she provided drinks, I spotted a chance to let them sample my wares. The cupcakes had gone down a storm and it had become tradition ever since.

'Have we got many collections today?' Bethany asked, returning to the counter.

'Two birthday cakes, three sets of birthday cupcakes and a golden wedding anniversary cake which I need to finish off.'

'Crumbs! How do you find the time to decorate so many cakes?'

'I don't watch TV, I have no boyfriend, and my best friend is currently posted in Afghanistan. I don't exactly have a crazy, busy social life, do I?' I tried not to sound bitter about it. I loved my job and wouldn't change it for the world, but I was very aware that it would be healthy to have a few activities in my diary which extended beyond a monthly business meeting and the occasional catch-up with Tara in her café after work. If only Liam hadn't left. I missed him so much.

Bethany rested her backside against the counter and slurped her tea. 'I still can't believe Liam joined the army. He was so small and weedy when you were at school together.'

'Yeah, well, he filled out. Late developer like me.'

'I always thought that you two would end up together,' she said.

'Liam and me?' I felt a blush starting to creep up my neck

towards my cheeks and bent my head, pretending to busy myself rolling an icing ball. 'Why would you think that?'

'You always seemed so close, as though it was just the two of you against the whole world and neither of you wanted or needed anyone else.'

'We didn't and it *was* us against the world.'

'It's crazy that you two were bullied at school for your looks. Look at you now! You're gorgeous and Liam's a hottie.'

'I don't know about gorgeous but thank you.' I looked up again, confident my cheeks were no longer ablaze. 'I need to crack on with this anniversary cake. Are you okay staying shop side?'

'Definitely. Shout me when you want another cuppa.'

I made my way into the storeroom and gathered together what I needed to decorate the cake. It was already iced and I'd created an elderly couple dancing to stand on top of it, but I had some flowers to make.

As I worked, Liam filled my thoughts. During the summer holidays between primary and senior school, his family had moved into Sundleby – the village where I lived on the outskirts of Whitsborough Bay. A short, skinny eleven-year-old, his long blond fringe covered his face, as though he was trying to hide from the world, and he moved with his shoulders slumped and his head hung low. I felt an affinity towards him from the moment I first spotted him in the village shop. I also used my dull, dark-blonde frizzy hair as curtains from the world. For some unfathomable reason, I'd never quite fitted in at primary school. I hadn't been bullied but I hadn't had friends. It was as though I was invisible. I smiled at the new boy but he simply stared at me from beneath his fringe then looked away.

I'd hoped my cloak of invisibility would lift when I started senior school but the first term was pretty much like the whole of primary school – a lonely existence off everyone's radar. Liam had made no impact either but, after he ignored me in the village shop, I couldn't bring myself to open up a conversation in case he rejected me once more.

I returned to school after the Christmas holidays sporting braces and suddenly I *was* on the radar – of Elodie Ashton, the worst bully in our year.

'Oh my God! Your family must really hate you,' she'd cried, plonking herself down at my table during lunchtime.

Her gang surrounded her, their expressions eager as they awaited the punchline.

'A mouthful of metal for Christmas?' Elodie continued. 'That's just mean.'

'What should we call her?' one of her friends asked.

My heart raced as Elodie considered for a moment before smiling triumphantly and raising her voice a notch to address more than just her friends. 'Everyone! I'd like to introduce you to Bear Trap.'

There were squeals of laughter all round me and I could hear the name travelling round the canteen like an echo. I slid down in my seat, wishing it would stop. But it didn't. All afternoon, I was taunted by chants of 'Bear Trap' and 'We're going on a bear hunt'.

As I walked home from school that afternoon, fighting back the tears, Liam fell into step beside me and spoke to me for the first time ever. 'Are you okay?' he asked, his voice full of concern.

'What do you think?' I snapped, increasing my pace.

'Sorry.' He raced after me. 'She shouldn't have said that.'

I shrugged. 'It's my fault.'

'How?'

'Have you ever heard the phrase "be careful what you wish for"?' I asked him. 'I wished I wasn't invisible and look what's happened. The whole school knows me now.'

Feeling weary, I slowed my pace and we walked in silence for a while.

'I never thought you were invisible,' he said eventually.

I stopped and turned to face him, my eyebrows raised. 'Really? After you first moved in, I smiled at you in the village shop and you saw me but you completely blanked me.'

He swept his fringe away from his forehead, revealing the most dazzling blue eyes which he fixed on my hazel ones. 'I didn't think you were smiling at me. Sorry. I'm used to being invisible too.'

We stood there for a moment, tentatively smiling at each other, recognising the loneliness.

A shout coming from the other side of the road tore our gazes away.

'Oh my God! Look!' Elodie screeched. 'Bear Trap's got a boyfriend. It's... it's... I've got it! Skindiana Bones.'

My stomach churned as her gang whooped and cheered. And that was that. The nicknames stuck and the bullying was relentless but Liam and I weathered it together, our friendship getting stronger and stronger as we became outcasts united.

As we moved into the final two years at school, the other boys in our year group grew taller, wider, and started to look like men but Liam seemed to have halted at 5 foot 6 and hadn't filled out at all. My braces had long gone although my nickname hadn't. I'd sprouted to 5 foot 8, but height was the only part of me that had developed. I had no waist, no hips and a flat chest. More fodder for the bullies.

The constant abuse – which sometimes turned physical – was tough to take. Schools approach bullying very seriously these days but, back then, we were told to 'just ignore it'. We didn't tell our parents what was going on for fear of more severe repercussions from the bullies if they took it further. Together, Liam and I struggled through each day.

We lived for evenings, weekends and school holidays when we could escape from the harassment and walk or cycle for miles up and down the coast, chatting about our plans for our future careers – Liam wanted to be an engineer and I wanted to be a chef – and a bully-free existence. We both secured a recurring part-time summer job in a café, working the same shift, and went camping on our days off. Life outside school really was an idyllic existence, spending every day with my best friend.

The day we finished school, Liam and I headed straight for North Bay and ran into the sea fully dressed, squealing as we soaked each other with cold, salty water.

'It's finally over,' he cried as we flopped onto the sand, drenched and exhausted.

'We're free,' I agreed, closing my eyes and taking in deep gulps of air. 'Five years of hell is over.'

Liam turned his head sideways and smiled at me. 'It wasn't all hell. I'd live through every insult and every beating again if it was the only way of having you in my life.'

I smiled back at him. 'Same here. You gave me far more than they took away.'

We lay there in silence, side by side, as the late afternoon sun dried our clothes and hair. I felt years of tension slipping away, as though each approaching wave grasped some of the hurt and pain and carried it out to sea, far away from me. Elodie had flunked her exams and was not going to college. Hopefully it was over.

During those summer holidays between school and college, extraordinary things happened to us both. Liam had a massive growth spurt taking him beyond 6 foot. His chest expanded and he discovered the gym, transitioning from lean to ripped. His face filled out and the dimples that had always been there were far more prominent, making his smile more alluring. My breasts finally developed and, inspired by Liam finally getting his long fringe chopped off, I had my hair thinned out and layers of light blonde and honey tones added in.

We started at technical college, me studying catering and Liam studying engineering as planned and, for the first time ever, we weren't invisible. We had new friends. We were noticed by the opposite sex. The first time I was asked out, I remember looking round the canteen, convinced it had to be a set-up.

Although we made new friends and even went out on the occasional date, Liam and I were still happiest together, walking or cycling up and down the stunning North Yorkshire Coast and going camping every summer. Nobody could make me laugh like Liam. Whenever I had news, my first thought was always, 'I can't wait to tell Liam that.' He made me feel so good about myself, as though I could achieve anything. A hug from him could chase my worries away, a look into those dazzling blue eyes could instantly comfort me, and his warm smile made everything better. It was no wonder boyfriends never lasted – every minute I spent with them was a minute I wasn't spending in my best friend's company. Liam had a few short-term girlfriends during our time at college and told me it was the same for him – time spent with me was far preferable. Outsiders often questioned our strong friendship and were convinced that it had to have gone further than that at some point. It really wound us both up. If we'd had a same sex friendship, nobody would have questioned it so why did us being the opposite sex automatically mean there had to be something going on? We were best friends and soul mates and that was that.

Two bully-free years at college flew past and we both secured apprenticeships to start in the September. At the beginning of our last ever long summer break, we went for a celebratory drink in The Old Theatre at the top of town. The pub was heaving with a mixture of locals and holidaymakers and there was no chance of a seat. The bar stools had been taken from round a high table so we rested our drinks on that.

A few drinks later, I leaned across the table towards Liam. 'Don't look now,' I whispered, 'but Elodie Ashton and the Biscuit Bunch are at my ten o'clock.'

'No! Do they still all look exactly the same?' he whispered. It was the reason why Liam had come up with the genius name, 'Biscuit Bunch', because the large group of girls had been carbon copies of each other at school, exactly like a packet of biscuits – same hairstyle, same way of wearing their skirt and tie, same coat, same shoes, same bag … and same merciless bullying.

I discreetly surveyed the group. 'Yep. Two years have passed and they're still biscuits. Ooh! Looks like Scarlett James may be expecting a baby biscuit.'

Liam laughed. 'Baby biscuit? Love it! You do realise it's killing me not being able to turn round, don't you?'

'Sorry. We can swap places in a minute.' I watched the group of eight girls laughing loudly and flirting with the men on the table next to them. Since leaving school, I'd occasionally spotted two or three of them round town – Whitsborough Bay wasn't big enough for our paths never to cross again – but I'd never seen them together as a big group. I'd wondered how I'd feel if I ever did and, surprisingly, there was no fear. There was no desire to flee from the pub. If anything, they seemed a bit pathetic in their matching short skirts and low-cut tops and caked-on faces, vying with each other to be the centre of attention.

'Do you know what's really strange?' I said, looking back at Liam. 'When we were at school, I used to think the Biscuit Bunch were the most beautiful girls I'd ever seen but, looking at them now, they're not that special. I don't mean that in a bitchy way. I just mean that they're not as dazzling as I remembered them. Even though I hated them for how they treated us, there was part of me that was in awe of them too. I actually wanted to be one of them.'

'You wanted to be in the Biscuit Bunch?' Liam smiled at me affectionately. 'You could *never* be a biscuit, Carls. You're an individual, not a clone. And you are – and always have been – far too stunning to be part of their group.'

I smiled at him. 'You're just saying that because you're my best friend.'

Liam reached for my hand across the table. 'I'm saying that because it's true.'

And there it was – the exact moment I realised I'd been in love with my best friend for years. Nobody else I'd met had held my interest because Liam already held my heart and I'd never even realised it. As I gazed into his eyes, my heart thumped so loudly that I half-expected everyone in the pub to stop what they were doing, turn round, and tell me to shush. The chatter seemed to fade into the background. It felt for a moment as though it was only the two of us and that what happened in the next few minutes could change our relationship forever. Unconsciously, I moved round the table, a little bit closer to him. He did the same, his eyes still fixed on mine, my hand still held in his. I could feel the tension crackling between us. Could he feel it too? Was he going to kiss me?

'Oh my God! Bear Trap? Is that you?'

Stomach sinking, I reluctantly looked away from Liam and met the curious gaze of the Chief Biscuit.

'It is, isn't it?' Elodie said, shaking her head in disbelief.

I nodded numbly, still reeling at the realisation about my feelings for Liam.

'Wow! You look so different. I almost didn't recognise you.'

I finally found my tongue. 'Hi, Elodie. You look nice.'

Elodie flicked her blonde spiral curls back from her face and straightened her dress in a way that suggested that she believed she looked more than simply 'nice'. She glanced down at the table where I was still holding hands with Liam then lifted her gaze to his face and widened her eyes.

'Skindiana Bones?' The surprise was obvious in her voice. 'That's never you?'

'No. It's Liam, actually,' he snapped. 'And this is Carly, in case you'd forgotten.'

Elodie grinned wickedly. 'Well, well, well. Life after school has certainly been kind to both of you. Most unexpected.'

'Yes, well, school *wasn't* kind to either of us.' Liam stared at her pointedly, a bitter edge to his tone.

'Oh, Liam, we were kids,' she purred. 'Don't take things to heart. It didn't mean anything.'

I nearly snapped, 'Maybe not to you,' but I didn't want to give Elodie or the Biscuit Bunch the satisfaction of knowing how much I'd been hurt by them, how it had taken most of college to rebuild the confidence they'd destroyed, and how I'd been up all night before starting college, throwing up, terrified that college would end up being just like school.

Elodie lowered her eyes back to the table again. 'So you two finally bumped uglies?'

Realising I was still holding Liam's hand, I snatched it away at the same time as he let go.

'We're just friends,' I protested.

'We're not together,' Liam said at the same time.

Elodie raised both her hands in the air in a surrender position. 'Okay. Calm down. I hear you.' She turned to Liam, smiling, and fluttering her long eyelashes seductively. 'If you're ever at a loose end, give me a call.' She produced an eyeliner from her handbag, lifted up his hand, and scribbled her mobile number on it. And all Liam did was stare at her, mouth slightly agape. I couldn't decide if he was shocked or mesmerised but, either way, I didn't feel comfortable.

My stomach lurched when Elodie stood up on her tiptoes and lightly grazed her red lips across Liam's. 'Don't be a stranger,' she said, stroking his cheek. Winking at me, she added, 'You snooze, you lose. See ya later, Bear Trap.'

'You're not going to ring her, are you?' I hissed when Elodie was out of earshot.

Brow furrowed, Liam slowly raised his fingers to his lips. 'She kissed me,' he muttered. 'The Chief Biscuit actually kissed me.' He didn't sound delighted but he didn't sound disgusted either.

'I know. I was right here. Are you going to wipe that off your hand?'

He looked down at the number and shrugged. 'Maybe later.'

My stomach sank. This could *not* be happening. One minute we were about to kiss – perhaps – and now he was thinking of asking the Chief Biscuit out. No! 'You're not going to call her, are you?'

'Of course not! Why?' He fixed his eyes on mine, his expression serious as he added in a gentle tone. 'Would it bother you if I did?'

*Yes! I want you to be with me!* But I couldn't bring myself to say the words. What if I'd misread that moment? What if it had simply been a few seconds of madness brought on by too many celebratory drinks? He'd had years to make a move and there'd never been the tiniest suggestion that he saw me as more than his best friend.

'I'm your best friend, not your girlfriend,' I muttered, aware of the stroppy edge to my tone. 'It's nothing to do with me who you choose to go out with.'

His eyes darkened. 'No, I suppose it isn't.'

And that was the moment – the crushing moment when I realised that I was going to lose him, that another woman was, one day, going to take him away from me. The brief relationships he'd had at college had been insignificant but he was a man now – a gorgeous, desirable one at that – and there was no way he'd stay single for long. I couldn't bear for him to be with someone else, because I wanted him to be with me forever ... and not just as my friend.

With an aching heart, I watched him staring at the number on the back of his hand, shaking his head slowly. He wouldn't call her. He wasn't that shallow. But somebody would come along and steal his heart and there was nothing I could do to stop them. I'd just have to stay quiet and hope that, one day, someone else would come along and steal mine because, for years, it had belonged to the young boy who claimed I'd never been invisible to him. The boy who'd turned into a man who, right now, wasn't seeing me at all.

Nothing happened between us after that and I had to accept that I'd imagined it and there hadn't ever been a 'moment' for Elodie to ruin. We spent the summer together; we went camping and our friendship was the same as it had always been.

In the September, we started our apprenticeships and our friendship didn't change but our routine did. I worked on Saturdays and Liam worked shifts so we couldn't see each other as often as before, although we tried our best.

It wasn't long before Liam had a steady girlfriend meaning our time together was even more sporadic. I started going out more with a couple of girls I knew from college and, on a night out clubbing, met Archie. He was perfect boyfriend material and, for two years, I tried so hard to let go of Liam and make it work but, every time I saw Liam, my heart raced and butterflies soared in a way they never did around Archie. It was only fair to let Archie go so he could find someone who wasn't already in love with their best friend.

Liam and I always met each other's partners but we never double-dated. Archie had once suggested it and the idea filled me with horror so I never proposed it to Liam and was glad he never raised the subject either.

When Liam and I were alone together, we'd ask how things were going but we never discussed our relationships in any depth. It became an unspoken rule that our time together was mainly about the two of us against the world, like it had always been. I loved that. In that world, I could pretend he loved me as much as I loved him.

The years passed and we settled into our jobs. My college friends both drifted out of my life after moving away from Whitsborough Bay, one for work and one for a relationship. Working in The Cake Shop alongside three women of advancing years did nothing to expand my social circle so, after ending it with Archie, my love life was pretty much non-existent.

One April morning when we were twenty-five, Liam texted me asking if he could meet me straight from work because he had something important to say. He'd been single for five months and I'd foolishly spent the day imagining he'd finally come to his senses and was going to declare his undying devotion to me. I was a bundle of nerves when he hugged me and suggested we walk down to the seafront. Walking barefoot along the shoreline, I anxiously waited for the words I'd longed to hear.

'I've been trying to say this for ages,' he said, his voice thick with nerves, 'but it's hard to find the words.'

My heart started thumping. 'You know you can say anything to me.'

'I'm scared it might hurt our friendship.'

That had to be it. He was finally going to say it. 'Nothing you say or do could ever hurt our friendship,' I assured him.

He turned to face me, clasped my hands in his and took a deep breath. I gave him an encouraging smile.

'I'm leaving Whitsborough Bay,' he said.

The smile froze on my face as a wave of nausea passed through me. 'You're doing what?'

'I've joined the army. I leave at the end of the month.'

He was leaving me? Never once in over fourteen years of friendship had Liam ever mentioned moving away from Whitsborough Bay, joining the army, and leaving me on my own.

'Why?' The word was barely audible above the lapping of the waves.

He shrugged. 'A chance to see the world.'

'But why now?'

He shrugged again. 'The time just felt right.'

'Don't leave me,' I begged.

'I have to.' He wrapped his arms round me and held me close to his chest as the tears tumbled. I'd lost him but not to another woman as I'd feared. I'd lost him to his career and there was nothing I could do to stop it.

A fortnight later, Liam left Whitsborough Bay and I felt like he'd taken a piece of me with him. I cried myself to sleep for weeks, mourning for my best friend and confidante, and mourning for the love I couldn't have.

Life had to go on, though. Our friendship became a distance one and I acknowledged to myself that I was going to have to get my act together and get over Liam because anything more than a platonic relationship was clearly never going to happen. But I was still waiting. And hoping. And wishing.

**4**

---

'Sarah and Nick are here,' Bethany called after we'd closed up that evening.

'Tell them I'll be two minutes,' I shouted.

I finished touching up my makeup as I listened to Bethany welcoming my friends into the shop. Sarah ran Seaside Blooms, the flower shop at the other end of Castle Street. She and her husband, Nick, had offered to help carry the cupcakes over to Castle Park ready for the Christmas lights switchon.

I pulled on my long, red winter coat and fastened the buttons, wrapped a soft navy-coloured scarf round my neck and pulled on my favourite green bobble hat. The temperature had dropped over the last few days and, although it was dry, it was cold.

'Thanks for helping,' I said, giving Sarah then Nick a hug. 'Saves us doing a couple of trips.'

I'd packed the cupcakes into eight large boxes. Directing them to grab two boxes each, I alarmed the shop, locked up, then led the way to Castle Park at the end of the street where several of the traders had already gathered with their friends and family.

'These look amazing,' Tara said as we placed a few open boxes on the tables she and her team had set up. 'I'm guessing from the quality that they're all your work and not Bethany's?'

I looked round to make sure Bethany was nowhere near.

'It's okay,' Tara assured me. 'She's at the other side of the tree with Sarah.'

'I had to do them all again,' I admitted. 'She made a mess of the few she'd tried, which was fine, but she managed to squirt butter icing over all of mine and ruined the lot.'

'Oh, Carly. When are you going to fire her?'

'I can't. She's my sister and she's great with customers. She's just not so great with cupcakes.'

Tara sighed. 'Never work with family. Too messy when it goes wrong. What are you going to do?'

'She's restricted to the shop side for the moment. She knows she's never going to master decorating and I think she's right there. She does feel bad about it, though, and I feel really sorry for her. This afternoon she told me that she doesn't want to help me with her wedding cakes anymore because she'll probably only screw it up.'

Bethany had chosen a simple white two-tier cake with a blue tartan ribbon and a few flowers on it. The guests would have cupcakes with a blue swirl topped with a white icing heart. I'd expected her to go for something grander but she'd been adamant that simplicity was key, joking that she didn't want to be outshone on her wedding day by a cake.

Tara poured coffees for a couple of the traders. 'From what you've told me, she probably *would* screw it up.'

'But it's her wedding and she was so excited about getting involved.'

'Every bride dreams of her perfect wedding day and Bethany obviously knows that her involvement in decorating the cakes would not lead to perfection. She's right to leave it to the professional.'

I sighed. 'I wish she could find something she's good at. She's always on about being a failure. She's got so—' But Bethany reappeared at that point, halting our discussion.

'Is your fiancé joining us tonight?' Tara asked her.

Bethany shook her head. 'He's meeting me afterwards. Wedding stuff.' She curled her lip up as though she'd said something really distasteful.

'I thought you'd have been really into all the wedding stuff,' Tara said.

Bethany sighed. 'I was at first. I liked trying on dresses and looking at venues, but it's all the detail I can't be doing with. There's so much to think about. We need to decide on our first dance and give the DJ a playlist. I'm going to be rubbish at it.'

'How can you be rubbish at picking music?' I asked.

'I can never remember the names of bands or songs. I told Joshua he'd be better off doing it without me but he insisted we do it together. Yet another thing to add to my rapidly expanding list of failures. Oh. That's my phone ringing.'

When Bethany stepped away from the crowd to answer her phone, Tara looked at me. 'Wow!' she said, wide-eyed. 'Where did all that failure stuff come from?'

I shrugged, a sinking feeling in the pit of my stomach. 'She's getting worse. I don't know what to do.'

A couple of traders appeared wanting drinks.

'We'll talk in the pub later,' Tara said.

Fifteen minutes later, drinks and cupcakes had been distributed to all the attendees. Falling silent, the small crowd turned and stared towards the far end of Castle Street, smiling and nudging each other as a loud cheer erupted from the direction of the main switch-on outside the shopping centre. Moments later, the lights at the other end of Castle Street illuminated for the first time this season, small sections at a time, rippling down the street like a river finding a new course. When they reached the end of Castle Street nearest the park, a curved banner declaring 'Welcome to Castle Street' lit up, followed by stars across the top and bottom of the banner. Seconds later, the white star at the top of the tree illuminated, followed by the tree itself. Red, green and white lights sparked into life to gasps of delight from the traders. As per tradition, everyone started singing 'We Wish you a Merry Christmas'.

I hugged Bethany to my side and smiled. I'd always felt out of place at school, and the insecurities from there meant I'd never fully settled at college. However, here on Castle Street, among the other independent retailers who'd made me feel so welcome, I'd found my place. I just wished that my little sister could find her place too.

* * *

'Tell me more about what's going on with your sister,' Tara said as we found a secluded corner towards the end of the evening. We'd been on a pub crawl down town with the other traders but the numbers had diminished by the time we'd made it to the seafront, settling in The Lobster Pot which overlooked the harbour in South Bay.

'She seems obsessed with being a failure at the moment and it's not just about her lack of cake decorating skills. It's putting a seating plan together, it's music choices like you saw tonight, it's pretty much everything. I'm not sure it's a new thing but it's certainly escalated recently and I'm worried it's my fault.'

Tara vigorously shook her head. 'It's not your fault she's crap at cake decorating. It's not like you haven't tried to train her.'

'Maybe I haven't tried hard enough.'

She shook her head again. 'And maybe she just doesn't have the aptitude for it. We're not all good at the same things. The best thing for your business is to have her resign or for you to let her go but we both know that you won't dismiss her and you won't accept her resignation. Your only other option is to do what you did today by keeping her on the shop side and look for someone who *does* have the talent. Thing is, you'll be paying two salaries that way when you only need one person.'

I sighed. 'You're right. It's a mess but she's my sister and she's clearly got some serious self-esteem issues right now. I'm going to have to do what I can to big her up for the things she does well like upselling to customers and try to keep her away from anything that could result in chaos.'

Tara took a sip of her wine. 'Is there really nothing she can do to help you with the cakes?'

'She can bake but that's it. She can't even sprinkle glitter across a tray of cupcakes. Somehow, some end up completely coated in the stuff and some have none and, of course, it goes everywhere.'

'You're going to have a fun December,' Tara said, grimacing.

I rolled my eyes at her. 'Aren't I just? But if I can make it through December, I can make it through anything.'

'Cheers to that.' Tara clinked her glass against mine and we changed the subject, but I felt unnerved. I'd flicked through my order book this afternoon and I wasn't sure I would make it through December without help. Not without surviving on only a few hours' sleep a night.

'So what are your Christmas plans?' I asked, keen to change the subject.

'Non-stop work serving the hordes of Christmas shoppers then two days of peace and quiet before sales madness brings them all out en masse again.'

I smiled. 'I don't mean at work. What are you doing on Christmas Day and Boxing Day?'

'Lot of options but nothing finalised yet.' She gulped down the last couple of mouthfuls of wine. 'Same again?'

Before I had a chance to respond, she was out of her seat and heading towards the bar. I slowly shook my head as I watched her lean over the bar to place an order. She'd done this before. Even though I'd known Tara for over four years, I often felt as though I didn't know her at all. She was warm, friendly and exceptionally supportive. She'd happily chat for hours about our businesses and customers but, as soon as the conversation steered away from work, she clammed up, changed the subject or found some other distraction like just now.

I still classed her as a good friend and loved spending time with her but our friendship was the opposite of what I was used to with Liam. I knew everything about him yet knew so little about her. She hailed from London and I knew that her family were still there but that was the only insight I had into her life beyond The Chocolate Pot. I had no idea why she'd left London and moved to Whitsborough Bay or what her life had been like down south. I knew nothing of past relationships or her hopes for the future. But did I need to? Not everyone was an open book like me. I smiled to myself. Who was I kidding? I wasn't an open book either. I'd never told Tara – or anyone else – how I felt about Liam. It seemed we both had our secrets. Perhaps it was time to share mine with Tara. Her business advice had always been sound; perhaps her relationship advice would be too. And maybe it would prompt her to open up to me.

She made her way back towards me with a couple of large glasses of wine and placed them on the table. 'I've ordered in some new sample hot chocolate flavours,' she said. 'Would you like to be my objective taste tester when they arrive?'

I smiled at her. 'I'd love to be. Thank you.'

And that was it. Subject changed again. As we chatted in the pub for another hour and then walked back up to Castle Street together it struck me that, despite Tara's avoidance of certain subjects, we never struggled for conversation. If that was the way she wanted things to be, I was happy to go along with it. I valued her friendship far too much to keep pushing and risk pushing her away. Maybe one day she'd feel ready to talk and I'd be there for her when she did.

# 5

THREE WEEKS UNTIL CHRISTMAS

'Morning!' Bethany sounded cheerful when she arrived for work on Monday morning, which filled me with relief.

'How was the weekend?' I asked, looking up from the unicorn-themed cake I was decorating for a 6$^{th}$ birthday.

'Lovely, thanks. Joshua took me out for a surprise meal at Le Bistro on Saturday night. It was just what I needed.' She hung her coat up.

'Dare I ask? Have you decided on a first dance?'

'She smiled. 'Yes, all sorted. We had a lazy day at home yesterday and did the music thing then instead of Saturday night. It was so much easier being able to listen to the songs and check all the lyrics were suitable. I've promised Joshua I'll keep it secret, though, so my lips are sealed.'

'I'll look forward to the surprise.'

I continued to cut out pink and purple glittery stars while Bethany made drinks.

'I'll stay shop side all week if that's okay with you,' she said, handing me a mug of tea a few minutes later.

'Okay. Thanks.' It was the best thing for both of us and for the business.

* * *

Over the next few days I listened carefully to each of Bethany's customer interactions, keen to find opportunities to praise her and hopefully build her confidence. It was very enlightening. I'd known she was good with customers but it was clear that she had a natural gift for opening up a conversation with everyone who came in, whether it was about the weather, their Christmas preparations, or how much she liked something they were wearing. Yet, at the same time, she efficiently served them. She never put her fingers in the icing or dropped any cakes on the floor which was strange because any time I asked her to fill a box of cupcakes ready for a customer collection, there were casualties. It seemed that whenever she was assigned a task she got worked up, convinced herself she was going to fail, became clumsy and dropped something making the failure a self-fulfilling prophecy. However, when she was relaxed, chatting to a customer, she showed no signs of clumsiness.

Each time I overheard her talking a customer into buying more cupcakes than they'd come in for or promoting the celebration cakes side of the business, I went out of my way to thank her. It was usually met with a confused shrug and a claim that she'd done nothing special but I kept doing it and hoped each positive affirmation would help convince her there were things she was good at.

Thursday arrived with solid torrential rain which hammered against the window, bounced off the cobbles and ran down the street in a fast-flowing stream. The bell barely tinkled all day which was hardly surprising. It definitely wasn't the weather to be out shopping, particularly buying cakes.

Even though Bethany must have been bored with so few customers, she insisted on staying in the shop and keeping quiet so I could focus on my orders. I spent the day in the workshop decorating a gorgeous cross-eyed cartoon penguin-shaped fruit cake working from a design a customer had given me. The penguin wore a pair of reindeer antlers which had become knotted in a string of colourful fairy lights. He held a sign stating 'Merry Christmas' and was standing in a snow scene adorned with candy canes and sweets.

'Oh my goodness, you are simply *the* cutest thing ever,' I told him as I stuck the final snowflake onto one of his antlers then stepped back to admire my work. He reminded me of Bethany. She somehow managed to get tangled up in the fairy lights every Christmas. 'Stay right there so I can take your photo as soon as I've cleared up.'

I placed my icing utensils and cutters into the washing up bowl in the kitchen then grabbed a cloth and wiped down the table. I positioned the penguin in the middle of the table ready for his photo shoot for my website and social media. Showcasing orders was a great way to bring in fresh business, although I never posted any photos until I'd checked with customers when it was safe to share. I didn't want to spoil any surprises.

I'd only taken one photo when Bethany appeared in the archway, her expression serious.

'What's up? I asked.

'Customer,' she said, biting her lip.

'And...?'

'And he's asking for you.'

'And...?'

She winced. 'And it's Jasper.'

My stomach sank to the floor. 'I don't suppose there's any chance there's another Jasper?'

Bethany shook her head. 'Sorry.'

Sighing, I removed my apron and checked myself in the kitchen mirror to make sure I didn't have icing sugar on my face or in my hair. Jasper Hargreaves. The man who'd broken my heart. Exactly what I didn't need right now.

At the start of the year after Liam left for the army, I decided it was time to move on. I gave online dating a go but lurked for a month or so, not feeling brave enough or confident enough to respond to any messages I received. Then, in early March, Jasper got in touch. I can't remember now what he'd said in his opening message but I remember it making me laugh out loud. It struck me that I hadn't done that since Liam left, which saddened me. If this Jasper – an absolute stranger – could amuse me like that, then he was worth getting to know a little better.

After a few days of exchanging messages, we arranged to meet in The Lobster Pot. I knew that the immediate physical attraction to Jasper came from his resemblance to Liam – messy blonde hair, bright blue eyes and dimples. He could make me laugh and, like Liam, he worked with his hands in his job as a carpenter. He wasn't Liam but he was definitely the next best thing.

We had a great relationship and I grew to care for Jasper deeply. The problem was that, every time I felt that I could finally let go of Liam and fully throw myself into my relationship with him, Liam would come home for a visit and I'd be back to square one, hopelessly devoted to him. We'd meet up and it would be just like old times, walking or cycling up and down the coast, chatting incessantly about life, the universe and everything. Everything except relationships, that was. His time in Whitsborough Bay was so short that I never introduced him to Jasper and I didn't have the opportunity to meet his girlfriend, Aimee, who was also serving in the army, because she spent leave with her family rather than coming to Whitsborough Bay.

One freezing cold March day, two years into my relationship

with Jasper, I saw a Facebook update from Aimee that turned my world dark. I wasn't friends with her on Facebook but she'd tagged Liam into the post which meant I heard their big news via social media rather than directly from him: *So excited! Finally moving in with my gorgeous man xx* There was a photo of them in their uniforms outside their new army quarters. They looked so happy. Staring at that picture, I had to accept that it was properly over for Liam and me. He had a new life away from Whitsborough Bay which didn't include me as anything more than a friend and it was time I accepted that. For the first time ever, I doubted he valued my friendship that much anymore. We'd never talked about our relationships in detail but we'd always been honest about our relationship status. Moving in with Aimee was huge news and wouldn't have just happened overnight. Why hadn't he told me? Why had he let me find out like this? It was time to move on and give my all to Jasper.

That night, I stayed over at Jasper's house like I often did. Although I'd opened Carly's Cupcakes the year before, I'd continued to live at home, rent-free, at Mum and Dad's insistence. They'd suggested that renting out the flat above the shop for a year would bring in extra valuable income during my first year of trading. I couldn't argue with that logic or their generosity but, at twenty-eight, I felt a bit old to be still living with my parents.

Snuggled up next to Jasper in bed, I broached the subject of moving in with him and felt him tense.

'Can't we just keep it as it is?' he asked, lightly stroking my arm. 'I thought things were going well between us.'

'They are,' I insisted. 'And when things are going well, that's usually a good time to take the next step.'

He stopped stroking. 'Which is moving in, is it?'

I flinched at the clear disinterest in his tone and twisted round to face him, my stomach churning. 'Is me moving in really such a bad idea?'

He sighed. 'No, but it won't stop there, will it? It's never just moving in. It's a complete loss of independence. It's re-organising your life to suit someone else. It's marriage and kids. It's a lifetime tied down to one person.'

I stared up at him in disbelief. Where had that come from? He'd never said anything to suggest that moving in, marriage and kids weren't where we were heading. Although he'd never said anything to suggest they were, either.

'Please don't look at me like that,' he said, gently. 'Can't we just forget this conversation ever happened?'

Swallowing the lump in my throat, I edged away from him. 'You don't want marriage or children?'

'Absolutely not. And don't get mad with me because I've never claimed I do.'

'I just assumed...' I tailed off. What an idiot I'd been. For the past two years, I'd been so preoccupied with trying to get over Liam and channel my feelings onto Jasper instead that I hadn't paused to notice that he hadn't fallen in love with me. And the irony was that, at that moment, knowing I'd just lost him, I realised I *had* fallen in love with Jasper somewhere along the way. What a mess!

'What if I want those things?' I asked tentatively, pulling the duvet protectively round me, knowing already that it was over but not wanting to believe it.

Jasper looked at me with sad eyes. 'Then it's probably time to call it a day so you can find someone who also wants those things. Sorry.'

'Can't we even talk about it?'

He shrugged. 'What's the point? I won't change my mind.'

'Do you love me?' I asked.

'Of course I do. Just not enough to—'

'Yeah, I get it.' I flung the duvet back and yanked my T-shirt over my head, frustrated with him and furious with myself. 'Just not enough to live with me or stay with me or have any sort of future with me. Cheers for that, Jasper.'

'Carly! Don't be like that.'

I pulled on my jeans. 'How do you expect me to be?' I cried. 'I've wasted two years on you, Jasper. Two years.'

'It's not my fault,' he snapped. 'If you'd bothered to ask me what I wanted, you'd have known that my future plans have never and will never include marriage or kids.'

Six months later, I heard through a mutual friend that Jasper had walked up the aisle with Andrea Cleaver and I moved into the flat above the shop, heartbroken. Five months after that, the same friend told me that Andrea had given birth to a baby boy. The moment I closed the shop that day, I stumbled up the stairs, threw myself on my bed, and cried until the early hours.

'Good luck,' Bethany said, bringing me crashing back to the present.

I took a deep breath and rolled my eyes at my sister. 'I guess I'd better see what he wants. Could you do me a favour and take some photos of the penguin ready for social media?'

'Of course.' She took my phone from me.

'You don't need to touch him. Just move around him and get him from different angles.'

'No problem. Even I can't make a mess of that.'

'Jasper!' I said brightly, making my way through the archway and giving him a dazzling smile. It had been more than three-and-a-half years since we'd split up and I didn't want him to think I harboured a grudge or still carried a torch for him even though he looked just as gorgeous as I remembered and there was a momentary stirring of butterflies in my stomach. 'What an unexpected treat. How's married life and fatherhood treating you?' My cheerful tone suggested a confidence I didn't feel.

Jasper grimaced and shuffled awkwardly. *Good. He should feel uncomfortable, the liar.*

'Sorry about that,' he muttered. 'I really didn't want any of those things until...'

'Until the right person came along,' I finished when he faltered. I shook my head. 'Water under the bridge. So what brings you here, especially on a day like this, dripping all over my lovely floor?'

Jasper looked at the puddle of rainwater at his feet and shrugged apologetically. 'I've got a cake-related emergency and I'm hoping you can help.'

'I kind of guessed that much. What's the problem?'

Jasper visibly squirmed. 'It's our daughter's christening and the caterer has let us down.'

My stomach did a somersault. 'You've got two kids now?'

'Actually, Thea's number three.'

Ouch. I shook my head. 'I can't help you, Jasper.'

'Can't or won't?' he challenged.

I glared at him. The butterflies had ceased flapping their wings and now I felt annoyed. 'A bit of both.'

He nodded his head and turned as if to go, but his emergency was obviously too great. 'Please, Carly!' he said, turning back towards me. 'I know it's awkward because of what happened but I'm desperate. I wouldn't have come here if I wasn't.'

'Thanks a lot.'

His already flushed cheeks turned crimson and he looked mortified. 'I didn't mean it like that. Your cakes are delicious and you're very talented. You know I think that. But the christening's on Sunday. We've been let down and nobody else will make us a cake at such short notice.' His voice was so full of pleading that I half expected him to drop to his knees and beg.

'Do you remember how long it takes to decorate a decent cake?'

'Hours and hours but please, Carly. Andrea's in a right state about it.'

'Why's that my problem?'

'It's not, but please! I'm begging you. I know I treated you badly and I really am sorry, but we're talking about a baby here. Thea will never have another christening day.'

I couldn't help but feel sorry for him as he stood there looking like a drowned rat, his hair plastered to his head and his coat clearly drenched through. He looked at me with the sad puppy dog eyes that I used to find hard to resist.

'Oh for God's sake,' I snapped. 'Stop with the guilt trip. What sort of cake were you meant to be having?'

Jasper scrolled through his phone and showed me an image of a complicated two-tier pink and white cake. A teddy bear sat on the top and cupcakes positioned round the bottom each bore an intricate design.

'No chance,' I said, pushing his phone away. 'Sorry, Jasper, but I have a business to run and, in case you hadn't noticed, it's Christmas. I have a stack of Christmas cake orders alongside everything else. Even if I didn't sleep, I wouldn't have time to fit in a cake like that. Sorry.'

His whole body slumped. 'Oh well, it was worth a try. Thanks anyway.' He turned to leave. 'I just thought that, if anyone could do it, you could. It was wrong of me to come here after how things ended between us. I'm sorry. We'll just have to get Thea christened without a cake.'

A battle raged inside me. I wanted to prove to Jasper that he hadn't hurt me so much that I couldn't accept his business but I hadn't been lying about the lack of time to squeeze the cake in. I pictured a girl version of Jasper in several years' time looking at her christening photos and asking in a mournful voice why there was no cake.

Jasper reached out for the door handle.

'Wait!' I called, cursing myself for being such a sucker for a sob story.

He turned round, hope in his eyes. 'You'll do it?'

'Yes, but not *that* cake. No chance.' I raised my voice. 'Bethany? Have you finished with my phone?'

She wandered into the shop and handed it over. 'All done,' she said.

'Thanks for doing that.' I located the christenings' album on my phone and scrolled through the images until I found the one I wanted.

'I can do you this.' I thrust a simple image of a two-tier pink and white cake with some hearts, flowers and footprints on it. 'If you want, I can put a small teddy bear on the top instead of a bow, but I don't have time to do anything fancier than that. Final offer. Take it or leave it.'

Jasper smiled. 'I'll take it. Thank you. When can I collect? Saturday morning?'

I gave him a sarcastic laugh. 'Don't push your luck. I'll still be working on it on Saturday night. You can collect it from here at eight o'clock on Sunday morning, not a minute sooner, not a minute later.'

I handed him a pad and pen from beside the till. 'Write your number down here and I'll text you with the price.'

'It's the same number as before,' he said.

'And I deleted it so write it down again please.'

As I watched him scribble down his number, a smug grin on his face, I couldn't help feeling I'd just been manipulated big time. Two could play at that game.

'It'll cost you extra because of the rush-job,' I declared.

He finished scribbling and looked up. 'I'm not worried about the money. I just need the cake.'

'Can I interest you in any cupcakes while you're here?' I asked, smiling sweetly. 'Or perhaps you'd like to place an order for your wedding anniversary or one of your three children's birthdays.'

'I really am sorry,' he said.

I nodded and inclined my head towards the door to indicate that it was time for him to leave.

'See you on Sunday, eight sharp,' he said, before opening the door and heading out into the rain once more.

Bethany wrapped her arms around me. 'You did well.'

'He has three kids,' I said, resting my head on her shoulder. 'The man who didn't want marriage or kids has done marriage and *three* kids.'

'He wasn't right for you,' she said.

'I know he wasn't.' I stood up straight and stretched. 'I guess I'd better move onto my next Christmas order if I'm going to fit in a christening cake before Sunday.'

'You'll meet Mr Right one day,' Bethany called as I made my way into the workshop.

'I already have,' I muttered under my breath. 'I met him when I was eleven.'

# 6

---

The following Monday, I yawned and took a slurp of my fourth coffee of the morning before returning to my job of rolling white icing balls in various sizes. I could definitely have done without the addition of that christening cake for Jasper. It had massively set back my schedule and I'd ended up working until the early hours of Sunday morning finishing it.

My current project wasn't due to be collected until Friday but it was the most detailed Christmas cake I'd taken an order for so far this year, ordered by one of my regular customers for her son's seventh birthday party that weekend. It would be a five-tier cake alternating between vanilla sponge and chocolate cake. The first four tiers were to be set at jaunty angles so that, once joined together, they'd look like a mountain. A snow-covered road would travel to a cute little house on the top layer. Setting off up the path would be Santa pulling a sleigh full of toys, followed by a reindeer on skis. Playful penguins, snowmen, Christmas trees and candy canes were dotted along Santa's route.

Although I wouldn't bake the cakes until later in the week to ensure they were as fresh as possible, I needed to have the large number of individual components ready. I'd made Santa, the reindeer and the sleigh already and, considering how tired I was, the round balls for the snowmen and snowballs all the way up the mountain road were an easy task until I could wake up properly.

Bethany had booked the day off to do some Christmas shopping which couldn't be better timing because it meant that I could get my head down and catch up.

When the doorbell tinkled, I put down the icing ball I was rolling, wiped my hands on my apron and wandered into the shop.

'Tara!'

Tara smiled and thrust a large paper cup towards me. 'I come bearing gifts. Those new hot chocolate samples I was telling you about have just arrived. First up is salted caramel and I want to know whether you think it's worth stocking.'

I sniffed the drink through the gap in the lid. 'If it tastes as good as it smells, you're onto a winner.'

'I love it but, you know me, anything chocolatey and I'm sold.' She narrowed her eyes at me. 'I hate to say it, but you look shattered.'

I grimaced. 'I am. Remember my ex, Jasper? I was up till about 4.00 a.m. on Sunday decorating a christening cake for his daughter.' I quickly filled her in on Jasper's cake-emergency and his expanding family.

Tara slowly shook her head at me, her mouth set in a thin line. 'You're a better person than I am. After the way he treated you, I'd have told him where to shove his last-minute cake request.'

I smiled, imagining her doing exactly that. 'I tried to but then I felt sorry for him. I charged him extra, though.'

'I should think so too.' She cocked her head on one side and gave me a sympathetic look. 'How was it seeing him again?'

'Weird. The good news is that I didn't fancy him anymore. I had momentary butterflies but they didn't last long. I think it was just the surprise of seeing him again. The problem was after he left. The whole time I was working on the damn cake, I found myself replaying our relationship and managed to feel stupid and humiliated all over again that we split up because he told me he didn't want marriage and kids—'

'And then married and had kids with the next woman he met?' Tara interrupted. 'You're bound to feel that way but try not to think of it as a failure and more of a lucky escape. He wasn't the one for you. It was better that you found that out sooner rather than later, freeing you up to find the right person for you.'

'Great job I've done of that,' I said, sniffing at the hot chocolate again. 'I've been on a handful of unsuccessful dates since we split up whereas Mr No Marriage and No Kids has become a dad three times.' I took a sip of the drink. 'Oh my goodness, Tara. This is like heaven in a cup.'

'You like it?'

I took another sip and nodded. 'Definitely. I think you should—'

But I didn't get to finish the sentence because the door burst open and a very angry-looking woman stormed up to the counter.

'Thanks a lot,' she shouted. 'That cake was meant to be a secret.'

Tara took a couple of steps back from the customer, looking shocked.

'The penguin cake?' I asked, recognising the customer as Joanna Osborne.

'Yes, the penguin cake. She's seen it now. The secret's ruined. What the hell were you playing at?'

My heart raced. I couldn't bear confrontations. 'I don't follow...'

'I told you that it was a surprise.' Joanna's voice shook with anger. 'I told you not to show anyone but you showed the world. How unprofessional can you be?'

I took a deep breath and fought the strong urge to flee through the workshop and up the stairs to the safety of my flat. 'I can see you're annoyed but I genuinely don't know what you're talking about. The only person who's seen that cake, other than me, is my sister but she works here. I haven't shown it to anyone else.'

She planted her hands on her hips. 'Then how do you account for all the likes and shares?'

'Likes and sh... Oh no! Are you saying it's on Facebook?'

'Facebook, Twitter and Instagram, I believe.'

I felt the colour drain from my cheeks and grabbed onto the counter for support.

'Are you okay?' Tara rushed round to my side of the counter and placed a steadying hand against my back.

I nodded slowly. 'Just a bit shocked.' I looked up at Joanna. 'I'm so very, very sorry. It's all my fault. I asked my sister to take photos of the cake while I was with a customer and she must have posted them online, thinking she was being helpful.'

'Well, your sister's ruined everything.' Joanna's voice had lowered but she was still clearly livid. 'My daughter drew that penguin for her Art exam. She's had a rough time lately and I thought that seeing her imagination come to life as a cake would really cheer her up. Instead, she's been in tears because she's seen it online and now her friends have accused her of copying it and she's worried she's going to fail her exam.'

'I can't apologise enough. I can either take the images down or I can amend them to clearly state that the cake was made from an original design by your daughter.'

She glared at me.

'And you can have the cake free of charge, if you still want it,' I added hastily.

Joanna thought for a moment. 'I was going to tell you where to stick your penguin but free of charge, you say?'

I nodded. 'On one condition. Please don't put negative

comments about me or my business on social media and, if you've already done so, please remove them.'

I could tell from the way she flinched that she'd already vented her disgust online.

'It's a good offer,' I prompted.

She drew in a deep breath and stared at me for an excruciatingly uncomfortable moment, then relaxed her shoulders, took her phone out of her bag and tapped a few buttons. 'Okay. I accept. I've removed my comments.'

'Thank you. What would you like me to do with my posts?'

'Edit them to say the cake's an original design by Trinity Osborne.'

I nodded. 'Would you like to wait while I do that?'

She pursed her lips and shook her head. 'No. I've got better things to do with my time but if they're not amended in ten minutes, my comments will return.'

'They'll be edited as soon as you've gone.' I gave her a weak smile. 'I'm very sorry again. Would you like to take the cake now?'

'No. It's not convenient. I'll send my husband in first thing tomorrow as originally planned.'

With a swish of her long coat, she stormed out of the shop.

Tara looked at me admiringly and clapped. 'Well played, Ms Travis, well played indeed.'

'Except for the free cake.'

Tara shrugged. 'You've got to do what you've got to do. I'd have tried a discount but I'm not sure that would have worked. She was a tough cookie.'

I closed my eyes for a moment. 'I feel sick. I can't bear things like that.'

'Me neither. You know what you have to do now, though, don't you?'

'Edit those posts?'

'After that. You've got to fire your sister. I know she's got self-esteem issues but this is your business, Carly. She's costing you money.'

I held my head in my hands and groaned. 'You're right. I know you're right. I just don't know if I can do it.'

'You can! You've made a cake for your ex and you've placated a madwoman so you can find the courage to sack your sister. I've got to get back. Next time I see you, I want you to tell me that Carly's Cupcakes is a solo operation again and recruiting for someone who can actually add value to the business instead of taking it away.'

I said goodbye then took my hot chocolate into the workshop to sip on while I accessed my social media accounts and changed the messages, squirming at the enormous number of likes and shares but feeling relief that Joanna Osborne's comments had definitely been deleted. I didn't want to know what she'd written.

'Oh, Bethany,' I muttered. 'Tara's right. Do you know how much money you've just cost me?' I wished I'd thought about the implications of working with family before I'd offered Bethany the job. All I'd thought about was helping my sister out, keeping her safe and how much fun it would be. I'd thought keeping her on the shop side would mean disaster was averted but this had been by far her most costly mistake yet, and not just in terms of time and ingredients. Joanna Osborne had been hopping mad and, if she had the confidence to be so aggressive to my face, what sort of tirade of abuse had she unleashed on social media? She'd removed her comments but how many people had seen them first? The thought terrified me.

# 7

'Bethany, I don't know how to say this. I'm really sorry but having you working here isn't working.' I shook my head as I moulded some black icing into the shapes needed for the penguins on my mountain Christmas cake the following morning.

'No. I've said "working" twice. Erm... let's see. Bethany, you know those pictures you took of the penguin cake? I know you were trying to be helpful but you shouldn't have shared them on social media. The customer tore a strip off me yesterday and it's all your fault.'

I shook my head again, sighing.

'Bethany, I need to let you go. It's not you, it's me. Argh! That sounds like I'm dumping her.'

I heard the door a few minutes later, immediately followed by Bethany calling out, 'Only me!' She walked through the workshop and hung up her coat, her expression sombre. Dread enveloped me. What now?

'You're not going to believe what I've gone and done,' she said, her voice cracking as tears pooled in her eyes.

I patted the chair beside me and she slumped down into it.

'I'd ordered these little jars of love heart sweets from Etsy to give out as wedding favours and they should have been here by now so I chased yesterday but the woman hasn't done them.'

'No! Why not?'

'Because I messed up the order,' she wailed. 'She makes personalised tags for them and only processes the payment when she's got the details she needs for the tags. She'd sent me several emails asking for the information but, because I'm so rubbish and disorganised, I never saw them. She doesn't have time to do them now so I've got no favours and no chance of getting any ordered and delivered in time. Joshua asked if the kids' favours had arrived yet. We'd picked out these jars of crayons and little colouring pads.' She shook her head. 'I'd placed the order but there'd been a payment problem so I've got no kids' favours either.'

She cradled her head in her hands. 'Why am I such a screw-up? I'm panicking now that I've forgotten a pile of other things.' She looked up again, tears now streaking her cheeks. 'Joshua let it slip to his mum and she's called an emergency meeting tonight to go through everything. So now I'm going to be called out on my failures in front of his parents.'

I reached across and hugged my sister. 'I'm sure it won't be like that. They probably just want to help. If there's anything else to be done, I'm sure you can sort it between you.'

Bethany pulled away from me. 'How? There's only ten days left and it's Christmas so everyone's busy.'

'The favours can soon be sorted. You can get something for the kids in town. It might not be in a little jar but there are loads of shops selling colouring books and packets of crayons. For the adults, what about Charlee's Chocolates up the street? I know she makes wedding favours. It'll be heart-shaped chocolates instead of sweets but does that matter? She might even have jars for them. So why don't you sort out your mascara smudges, put your coat back on, and go and see Charlee now? Even if you don't place an order this morning, you can go to Joshua's parents armed with ideas and prices.'

'How do you do it?' Bethany asked, knitting her eyebrows together.

'Do what?'

'Act so calmly all the time and think so logically?'

I shrugged. 'It's easier to do when you're on the outside of a problem. When you're in the middle of it, it's harder to get perspective.'

'There you go again, full of words of wisdom.' Bethany stood up. 'Are you sure you don't mind me nipping straight out? You can dock my wages.'

'It's fine. Off you go.'

When she'd gone, I slumped back in my chair. There was no way I could dismiss her now. She'd called herself a screw-up again and the last thing I wanted to do was let her know that she'd cost the business a large commission because that would probably tip her over the edge when she was clearly feeling very low. I'd have to keep her on the customer side, refrain from asking her to do anything out of the norm, and hope she eventually resigned out of sheer boredom.

After I closed the shop for the day, I dropped into The Chocolate Pot to seek Tara's advice on the latest development with Bethany over another delicious salted caramel hot chocolate.

'You're far too nice,' Tara said, shaking her head after I'd filled her in.

'I know. It's going to be my undoing.'

'*Never* work with family. Simple as.'

I nodded. 'I've certainly learned my lesson the hard way.' I stretched my arms and rolled my head to loosen the tension. 'I hope Bethany's all right. Charlee said she could do her some heart shaped chocolate favours on time and at a better price than her original Etsy order but Bethany was still agitated all day. I think she's scared of discovering what else she's forgotten and looking stupid in front of Joshua's parents tonight. They're not the easiest of people to please and they're not her biggest fans.'

'She has ordered the dresses, hasn't she?'

'Definitely. I was with her when she did that and the final fitting is booked in. Also she's getting the flowers from Sarah so I know that's in hand too.'

'And the cake's from you, of course.'

'Yes. And Joshua sorted the photographer and cars so I think the main things are okay but it's those little details that she's worried about.'

'Weddings are stressful, 'Tara said. 'I don't think anyone realises how much planning goes on behind the scenes until they plan their own and then they discover that it's not all about the big fairy tale day. The lead up to it is hideously stressful.'

'You sound like you're speaking from experience,' I said.

Tara looked down at her feet.

I gaped at her realising I'd just been given an extremely rare glimpse into her past. 'Oh my goodness! *You* were married? Who to? When?'

She stared at me for a moment then shook her head. 'It's nothing. Forget about it.' She picked up the mugs and took them over to the sink but I followed her, my curiosity piqued.

'Are you still married?'

'God, no!' She turned round, vigorously shaking her head. 'I shouldn't have said anything. You promise you won't tell anyone?' She looked terrified at the thought.

'I promise. How long ago was this?'

Tara sighed and seemed to deflate before my eyes. 'Another life-time ago. I was twenty-one and we didn't even make it to our first anniversary,' she said, her tone flat and distant. 'Marrying Garth was the biggest mistake of my life. Never again. I am now officially a jaded cynic who has given up on relationships.'

I shook my head, stunned at the revelation. She'd always been guarded but this was such a big thing to have kept secret. 'How is it that we've been friends for over four years and this is the first I've heard of a husband?'

'Ex-husband,' she corrected.

'Sorry. *Ex.*'

Tara turned back to the sink and filled it with soapy water. 'You're the first person in Whitsborough Bay who I've ever mentioned it to and I'd like it to stay that way.'

'My lips are sealed. Do you want to talk about it?'

She washed the mugs and I waited patiently for her to answer although her rigid stance suggested this was not a subject she wanted to discuss.

'Maybe one day,' she said, turning to face me again, 'but not tonight. You've got cakes to decorate and I have Pilates.'

'Okay. But just say the word and I'm ready with a listening ear.'

She gave me a grateful smile. 'Thanks. Anyway, going back to the original subject, what did Bethany say about crazy penguin cake lady?'

When I pulled a face, Tara rolled her eyes at me and tutted. 'Carly! I can't believe you didn't tell her.'

'I couldn't. Even if I'd toned it down and made out that the customer was mildly miffed instead of all guns blazing, she'd have latched onto the fact that she did something wrong again and, with the mood she was in this morning, I think she'd have resigned there and then.'

'And your problem would have immediately been solved.'

'And my baby sister would have gone through the rest of her life convinced that she's a failure at everything so we're back to square one and the reason I didn't dismiss her in the first place.'

'I'm not sure I could avoid a conversation like that.' Tara picked up a tea towel and dried the mugs. 'It would bubble up inside me and I'd end up blurting it out at the most inappropriate moment. Aren't you worried about doing that, or is it just me?'

I thought about all those years spent being in love with Liam yet never uttering a word. 'I know what you mean but, believe me, I've become an expert at avoiding conversations.'

Tara stopped drying and eyed me suspiciously. 'An expert at avoiding conversations, you say? That sounds like a story.'

'It might be.' I sighed. It was time to open up and see if she had any advice because clearly working through it on my own hadn't proved a successful strategy. *Deep breath. It's only Tara. She's a great listener.* 'You know my friend, Liam?'

'The cute one who's in the army?'

I nodded. 'I might have a bit of a crush on him.'

Tara raised an eyebrow. 'You *might* have?'

'Okay, so I *do* have.'

She smiled knowingly. 'And by "bit of a crush", you actually mean that you're madly and passionately in love with the guy?'

I grimaced as I squeaked, 'Yep.'

'Oh. How long?'

'Definitely sixteen years. Could be longer.'

'That's some super enduring crush.'

'Yep.' I ran my fingers through my hair and shook my head. 'Over the years, I've tried so hard to get over him but nobody compares, although Jasper came very close and I did fall for him in the end, although it turned out the feeling wasn't mutual. Story of my life.'

Tara rested against the sink and folded her arms, surveying me with a thoughtful expression on her face. 'How do you know the feeling's not mutual with Liam?'

'Because if anything was going to happen, it would have happened years ago. The closest we ever came was after we finished college but I can't pin my hopes on that. I mean, we didn't even kiss. It was just one of those pre-kiss chemistry moments, and it was over in a flash. After that, we didn't speak about it and we continued as before, the best of friends.'

'You *have* to tell him how you feel,' Tara said.

'Yeah, right.'

'I'm serious, Carly. If he's the one for you and has been for more than sixteen years, you need to tell him.'

'He's my best friend. I can't risk losing that.'

'But think of all the things you'd gain if he feels the same.'

I shook my head. 'He doesn't.'

'How do you know? He could be sitting in the army mess right now telling one of his mates about how he fell in love with his best friend a zillion years ago and is too scared to tell her in case it changes the friendship.'

The thought of that made me feel quite weak at the knees but I dismissed it immediately. 'Somehow, I doubt it.'

'Is he married?'

'No.'

'Seeing someone?'

I shook my head. 'He was living with someone – Aimee – but they split up a couple of years ago and he's been single ever since but serving overseas so just as unavailable. We've never talked about our relationships in any depth, but we do tell each other when we're seeing someone.'

She stared at me thoughtfully again. 'Right, that's it! Grab your keys. We've got work to do.'

'What sort of work?'

'Pilates can wait but your cake decorations can't so you're going to create your little bits of icing wizardry while telling me all about Liam. And we're going to hatch a plan because my Christmas wish is for the pair of you to get out of the friend zone and get it together.'

Feeling excited by Tara's obvious enthusiasm, I grabbed my keys from the table. 'You old romantic, you. I thought you said you were a jaded cynic who was done with relationships.'

'For me, I am. My experience with Garth killed any notions of romance in my life. It doesn't mean I don't believe that there's such a thing as true love and a little Christmas magic for other people.'

\* \* \*

'What if it ruins our friendship?' I asked Tara after I'd told her more about my friendship with Liam, detailed the 'moment' in The Old Theatre, and admitted that I couldn't see myself ever being happy with anyone but him.

'It'll only ruin your friendship if you let it,' she insisted. 'The way I see it, one of two things are going to happen. The first is that you tell him, he admits he feels the same, you both can't believe how many years you've wasted and you live happily ever after. The second is that he doesn't feel the same, but so what? You've believed that to be the case for the last sixteen or so years and you've managed to maintain a great friendship throughout that time, so why would that change? It might be slightly awkward at first, but he'll realise that things can continue as before because they always have done. You won't have gained anything, but you won't have lost anything either.'

I had to admit that it made sense. The next problem was when I might get an opportunity to confess my feelings. When I'd last spoken to him, Liam had said that he was hoping to be home for Christmas but no leave had been signed off yet so it was still a bit up in the air. Having him home for Christmas would be amazing. What had Tara said about believing in the magic of Christmas? Could Liam be my very own Christmas miracle? He'd certainly been the one thing I'd secretly asked Santa for every year since I was eighteen and had realised my feelings for him. It was about time the man in red finally delivered my wish.

When Tara left, I sat at the workshop table with a mug of tea and scrolled through my phone, smiling at all the photos of him or the two of us together. Every single one held a special memory and I ached to hear his voice. I glanced at the time but shook my head. With the time difference, it was the early hours of the morning in Afghanistan so he wouldn't appreciate being woken up by a Face-Time call. Instead, I took a selfie of me looking sad and sent it to him with the message:

✉ Anyone seen my bestie? Last spotted leaving W'bro Bay in Feb. Please send him home for Christmas xx

Moments later, my heart leapt as my phone started ringing with a FaceTime request.

'I'm sorry. Did I wake you?' I said, grimacing.

He smiled, flashing those gorgeous dimples of his. 'I was struggling to drift off and I saw your message. You working late again?'

I nodded. 'Another hour then I'm done for tonight. How's it going?'

'Busy day. A couple of pieces of kit weren't working so lots of improvising to do. I think—'

'Liam, man! Pipe down!'

Something wacked Liam on the side of the face and he grinned at me. 'Sorry, Carls. Got to go before Geordie hurls something harder than socks at me. Night.'

'Night.'

The call ended and I held the phone against my heart, trying to calm the fluttering. Tara was right. I had to tell him and, if he got leave at Christmas, I would. Definitely. Perhaps.

# 8

'How was the emergency meeting?' I asked as soon as Bethany had taken her coat off the following morning. She turned round to face me and I gasped. 'Your eyes!'

She raised her hands and gently dabbed at the dark bags. 'Are they still red and puffy?'

'I'm afraid so. Was it that bad?'

'Worse.'

She flung herself onto the chair next to me and bashed into the table, sending my beautifully crafted icing nativity characters tumbling in all directions. I fought hard against the urge to retrieve them and check the damage.

'It was hideous,' she wailed. 'It all got very heated. I'd forgotten a pile of other stuff like a chocolate fountain for the evening do and some boxes of bubbles and...' She shook her head and flapped her hands. 'There were a couple of other things but I can't remember what they were now. Anyway, when it came to light how many things I'd failed on, everyone was looking at me and they seemed to want some sort of explanation. Even Joshua looked annoyed and he *never* gets annoyed. I tried to explain that those things weren't important to me so they weren't at the forefront of my mind and that I'd done all the really important things like writing meaningful vows but I think that it came across as though I didn't care about getting married.'

'Oh, Bethany.'

She wiped at a fresh torrent of tears. 'Margaret accused me of only being with Joshua for his money.'

I clapped my hand across my mouth. 'She never did.' Joshua earned a good salary as a surveyor and, despite his age, had already made money from developing and selling on a small portfolio of properties.

'She did,' Bethany said. 'She said I wasn't good enough for her son and that she should have known that me flitting from one job to the next was an indication of how I'd be in a relationship, flitting from one rich, good looking man to the next.'

'What did Joshua do?'

'He was furious. He said he was disgusted that she'd had those thoughts in the first place and even more disgusted that she'd chosen to share them, especially when they knew exactly why I'd left the nursery. Joshua's dad, Damian, tried to calm things down but he couldn't make her unsay those words so we left. Joshua's parting words were, "We *will* be getting married next Friday but if you feel that way about my wife-to-be, then perhaps you shouldn't be there". I've caused a family rift, Carly.'

'Come here, you.' I pulled my sister to her feet and held her tightly while she sobbed.

The tinkling bell a few minutes later indicated the arrival of a customer so I reluctantly pulled away.

'I'll be okay,' Bethany whispered, shooing me into the shop.

Dealing with the customer as quickly and politely as I could, I returned to the workshop to find Bethany leaning over the kitchen sink, splashing cold water onto her face.

'You get on,' she said, pointing towards my partially-made – and now partially-destroyed – nativity figures. 'I'll make us a cup of tea and pull myself together.'

'If you're sure...?'

'I'm sure. Shoo.'

'How was Joshua this morning?' I called to her, while assessing the damage.

Bethany switched the kettle on then leaned against the kitchen units. 'Worried about me and still angry with his mum. He texted her to say that he thought we all needed another couple of days to calm down and that, if they had plans for Thursday night, they should cancel them because they needed to come round to our house, apologies at the ready, and sort this out.'

'That'll be fun.'

'Won't it just? Margaret's always been snooty and a bit cold, but she was never nasty so I assumed she'd accepted me and I'd grow on her, but obviously not. How am I supposed to get past what she said? I'll have to for Joshua's sake but I'm going to feel like she's watching my every move, waiting for me to say or do something to prove that she's right and I'm not good enough for her precious son.' She dropped teabags into a couple of mugs. 'You know what the worst part of it is? It's that she's right. Not about the gold digger thing, of course, but about me not being good enough for Joshua. Every day I wake up and expect it to be the day he realises that he's made a huge mistake.'

I twisted in my chair so I could fully face her. 'What do you mean?'

'*I* know that I'm useless, *I* know that I'm a failure, *I* know that I make a mess of everything and one day he'll realise it too and run for the hills.'

'Seriously, Bethany, you've got to stop it with this failure thing. How many times have I told you that you're not a failure?'

'I'm hardly a success story, am I?'

The sound of the kettle boiling saved me from answering the question for a moment. Bethany clattered the teaspoons around the mugs, then handed me my drink but she was too heavy-handed and it slopped over the table, all over the Angel Gabriel and baby Jesus lying in his manger.

'See,' she cried. 'I mess up *everything*! I'm so sorry.'

'It's fine. It's just a bit of icing.' I grabbed some kitchen roll and mopped up the tea and melting figures. 'I can do them again. I wasn't happy with them anyway.' I hoped my lie sounded convincing.

'I think I'd better go home.' Bethany tipped her tea down the kitchen sink then grabbed her coat and bag off the hooks.

There was no way I could let her walk out after that little speech, even though part of me was screaming out for her to leave before she damaged anything else. 'Don't go. I've got a job that I need you to do so I could really do with you staying.'

'Does it involve anything I can break or damage?'

'No.'

She hung her coat back on its peg. 'I'm listening.'

I wasn't sure where I managed to pull the idea of a stocktake from, but it seemed to placate Bethany who was quite happy to disappear into the storeroom with a clipboard and pen. It was totally unnecessary. I had an effective stock control system in place and knew exactly how much I had of everything but it would give her time to calm down and me time to think about what to do next.

As I started again on baby Jesus and his manger, I reflected on my conversation with Tara about Liam. I was 99 per cent convinced that I should go for it and tell him how I felt but that 1 per cent of doubt kept creeping in and I suspected that, if he was granted leave for Christmas, that 1 per cent would rapidly increase with each passing day.

# 9

'You look happier today,' I said when Bethany arrived for work on Thursday morning.

'Joshua's sorted everything out for the wedding.' Bethany hung her coat up. 'He paid his assistant to do a couple of extra hours work, phoning round places and nipping out to the shops. She's ordered everything I'd forgotten and a whole pile of other amazing stuff that never even crossed my mind. Her sister's a wedding planner so she's got loads of contacts plus a garage full of stuff we can hire. I can't tell you how relieved I am.'

'That's brilliant news.'

'Joshua wants to tell his mum that it was me who sorted it all out but I won't let him. He never lies and I'm not having him lie for me. I want her to like me for me.' She looked at me intensely. 'I can do that. I can bring her round. I'm good with people, aren't I?'

I gave her a warm smile. 'You're amazing with people.' I could say that with confidence and genuinely mean it.

She flicked the kettle on, singing softly to herself as she prepared the mugs. I returned to the Santa I was making, feeling as though we might have reached the calm at the other side of the storm. As long as Joshua's mum redeemed herself tonight, everything was going to be fine. Hopefully.

An hour later, my phone rang with a FaceTime request and my heart leapt when I saw Liam's name on the screen.

'Hi, how's it going?' I asked as soon as I accepted the call. As always, the sight of his wide smile and adorable dimples made my heart race faster and butterflies go wild in my stomach. And it hadn't gone unnoticed over the years how good he looked in army khakis, especially the pale desert-patterned one he was wearing right how.

'Hot and dusty,' he said, wiping his forehead to emphasise his point.

'It's minus one today,' I said.

He closed his eyes and smiled. 'Minus one? Sounds like heaven.' He opened his eyes again. 'I won't keep you long because I know you'll be busy. In fact, I bet you're rolling out some icing while we're speaking.'

I looked down at the table and laughed. 'I hadn't even registered I was doing it. You know me far too well. I've just made Santa's eyebrows.' I turned the phone so he could see the white curves resting on the table. 'Today's cake is an exhausted Santa fast asleep in his bed after delivering all the gifts on Christmas Eve.'

'I bet it'll look amazing,' he said as I turned the phone back to face me. 'What are your Christmas plans?'

'Bridesmaid dress fitting after work on Saturday, the wedding next Friday, then Christmas day with the parents. Other than that, non-stop work, although I can always find time in my demanding schedule if a certain person is coming home.' My heart thumped as I thought about seeing him in person again and possibly taking that next step, if I could muster the courage. 'Do you have news?'

'I do. I've finally got leave signed off and I'll be back in Whitsborough Bay on Monday.'

'This coming Monday? As in four days' time?' I only just managed to stop myself from squealing with excitement.

'That's the one. The flight's booked and my mum's already fussing round getting my old room ready.'

'Liam! That's amazing. How long will you be home?'

'Definitely for New Year and, after that, it depends.'

I was about to ask him what it depended on, but I could hear raised voices in the background and see him turning away from the camera.

'I've got to go,' he said, glancing back. 'I'll call you when I'm back. I'm dying to see you. Bye.'

'Bye, Liam.' But he'd already disconnected the call. 'I love you,' I whispered.

I put my phone down on the table and leaned back against my chair, smiling. I was dying to see him too. He'd last been home in February but it had been a fleeting visit before deployment to Afghanistan and we'd only managed one evening together where four hours had flown as quickly as four minutes. But now he was coming home for at least a fortnight. If I couldn't pluck up the courage to tell him how I felt during that time, I didn't deserve him.

* * *

Bethany stayed on the customer side of the shop for the rest of the morning, well away from my creations. She came into the workshop to make drinks intermittently but left mine next to the kettle, saying she didn't trust herself not to spill it and ruin something else. I didn't protest.

After lunch, she leaned against the archway, sipping from a cup of tea, watching me. 'You're so talented,' she said. 'It always amazes me how something that starts off as nothing more than a few blobs of icing can come to life in your hands and even ends up with a personality.'

I'd moved onto another nativity scene and smiled as I looked up from the king I was making. 'You really think they have personalities?'

Bethany nodded. 'Definitely.'

'That's a relief. I thought it was me going mad.' I'd always thought that the way I positioned the eyes and mouth created different personalities but was never sure whether that came across to others so it was lovely to hear that Bethany could see it.

While she watched, I attached the king's arms to his body and added in his gift of gold. 'I think that's everything needed for the nativity scene. Can you do me a favour and grab the container from the storeroom? It's already prepared.' I always made whatever was needed to decorate a cake – figures, stars, flowers, hearts and so on – in advance of baking the cake then stored them in a plastic container in the storeroom. Each container had a tick list of components and quantities taped to the front, ensuring I never missed anything.

The doorbell sounded while Bethany was in the storeroom so I went to serve the customer. When I returned to the workshop, Bethany was standing by the table with the plastic container for the nativity figures in one hand, a clipboard in the other, and a face like thunder.

'What the hell's this?' She held up the clipboard, eyebrows raised.

I winced. 'Oh.' When I'd sent Bethany to get the plastic container, it had never entered my head that my stock control folder was resting right next to it.

'Care to explain why you asked me to do a stocktake when you'd already done one?'

'You were so down about everything that I wanted to give you something to do that you couldn't m...' I trailed off as I realised what I was about to say.

'That I couldn't mess up?' Bethany suggested. 'So now my in-laws, my fiancé *and* my sister think I'm a failure. Thanks a lot, Carly.'

'I didn't mean it like that.'

She thrust the container and the clipboard at me and reached for her coat. 'I'm going out for a walk.'

'Bethany! Don't go.'

But she shoved past me and stormed out of the shop, slamming the door behind her.

I sighed as I shook my head. 'Nice one, Carly,' I muttered. 'You handled that *really* well.' I looked at my nativity figures lined up on the table. 'What are you lot looking at? If you've got any bright ideas, I'd be happy to hear them.' I glared at them for a moment. 'Don't all speak at once, guys.' I shook my head again and rubbed my tired eyes. 'I seriously need to get a life. I almost expected one of you to answer just then.'

The bell tinkled so I put the clipboard and container down on my chair and wandered into the shop, plastering a smile on my face. 'Hello. How can I help?'

'I'm here to pick up a cake for my mum, Joyce Wiseman. I think she said it's shaped like a snowman.'

'Ah, yes. It's all ready for you.'

As I showed the customer the cake in the shape of a large snowman wearing a purple and lilac striped hat and scarf and holding some Christmas gifts, I willed Bethany to walk back through the door. I willed her to return all afternoon but to no avail. I tried ringing her several times but my calls went to voicemail.

The shop was busy all afternoon with a combination of collections, orders being placed and customers treating themselves to one or more of the many Christmas cupcakes on offer. Apologising as a queue developed at one point, I cursed Bethany under my breath. Okay, so I'd got her to do an unnecessary piece of work but so what? It wasn't fair of her to storm out and leave me in the lurch. I'd really needed this afternoon free from serving to keep on top of the orders.

After I'd returned to the shop side six times in a row, getting no work done in the meantime, I picked up my phone and stabbed in a text:

✉ To Bethany
If you don't get your backside back to the shop in the next 10 minutes, don't bother coming back at all. It's been mayhem and I needed you. I'm hours behind on my orders now. Cheers for that!

My finger hovered for ages over the send button before I relaxed my shoulders and deleted the message. Instead I typed:

✉ To Bethany
I'm sorry about earlier. I thought I was help-ing. I hope it goes well tonight. Please come in tomorrow as I have lots of collections due and need your help xx

'She'd better show up tomorrow and with a damn good apology,' I muttered. 'Otherwise it's the end. It has to be.'

* * *

I crawled into bed past midnight, my eyes burning with fatigue, my stomach protesting with hunger, and my body aching from so many hours hunched over my table. Thanks to Bethany walking out and the preparation time I'd lost as a result, I'd had to bake and decorate until 11.30 p.m. I could have done with a couple of hours longer but I'd started to make careless mistakes so the time was no longer productive. I'd have to get up at the crack of dawn instead.

Bethany hadn't responded to my text so I had no idea whether she'd show up tomorrow or not but I hadn't the time or patience to call her and beg.

Even though I was fuming with my sister, the last person I thought about as I drifted off was Liam. Four more days and the love of my life would be back. It couldn't come soon enough.

## 10

TEN DAYS UNTIL CHRISTMAS

I was back in the workshop at 4.50 a.m. on Friday morning in a desperate attempt to catch up. My first task was a ruby wedding anniversary cake and 100 cupcakes. The cake was simple and classy: two tiers in white icing with a forty on the top and a flow of red hearts down the front. The iced cupcakes would each feature a heart or flower design. I'd baked the cakes last night and had prepared half the icing items but there was a lot still to do. If Bethany hadn't stormed out, I'd have done most of the work yesterday afternoon with only the finishing touches saved for this morning. This was not how I liked to work. It felt chaotic and unprofessional.

In an effort to calm myself, I put on a Christmas album and made a mug of hot chocolate before starting work. With the fairy lights twinkling in the shop and workshop, it wasn't long before I felt relaxed and Christmassy.

About forty-five minutes into cutting out the shapes for the cupcakes, I became aware of the light changing and looked up, frowning. Sunrise wouldn't be for another couple of hours. I stood up, stretched, and wandered into the shop.

'It's snowing!' I exclaimed, rushing to the window. Large white flakes tumbled from the pinkish sky. It hadn't rained since the day Jasper had ordered the christening cake so the snow was already settling on the dry cobbles. Mesmerised by the flakes, I stood by the window for about ten minutes before reluctantly tearing myself away and returning to the workshop.

Thirty minutes later, I put the kettle on again and wandered into the shop to see a thick blanket of snow had already covered Castle Street. As it was still only 6.15 a.m. and none of the businesses opened until 9.00 a.m., the street was deserted. The Victorian streetlights were on, casting a warm yellow glow over the crisp white snow.

'It's like a scene from a Dickens novel,' I said to myself, and I had a sudden overwhelming urge to be part of it. Running up to my flat, I dug out my boots and pulled on a jumper before dashing back down to the shop and grabbing my hat, scarf and coat.

Outside, I tilted my head back towards the sky and closed my eyes, letting the flakes gently kiss my face. I opened my arms wide and inhaled deeply. Repeating that several times, I felt the stresses of the past week ebb away.

When I opened my eyes, I looked down Castle Street to the end furthest from my shop, where it connected onto the main precinct. All that fresh, perfect snow. There was only one thing for it.

I locked the shop door then ran down my side of the street, my coat billowing behind me. I ran all the way to the far end then back again on the other side. Red-cheeked and gasping for breath, I paused outside my door. I looked back at my footprints in the snow on both sides of the street and smiled as I thought of Liam and I first-footing in Farmer Duggan's field. It had been about a week before Christmas, just like it was now, and we'd been in our final year of senior school at the time. Despite the weather forecasters claiming there'd be no snow until the New Year, it had fallen steadily all day creating a buzz of excitement in lessons. By home time, there'd been about a foot of snow and drifts of up to three feet. Liam and I had walked home together as usual. The journey took us past some fields belonging to Farmer Duggan, a friend of Liam's dad's. We'd both glanced at the first field.

'Look at that untouched snow,' I'd said. 'I'd love to first-foot in that.'

'Very tempting,' Liam said, smiling.

There was a stile in the stone wall surrounding the next field. Liam nudged me then threw his backpack over it. 'Last one in buys sweets tomorrow!'

He leapt over the stile with me hot on his heels. We raced round the field in opposite directions, meeting at the top and running down the middle together, hand in hand, giggling helplessly.

'I've never done this before,' I said, throwing myself onto my back in the deep snow in the centre of the field and swishing my arms and legs apart. 'I've always wanted to.'

'Snow angels?' Liam exclaimed. 'Neither have I.'

He threw himself onto his back beside me and the two of us lay there, creating angels in the fresh snow, still giggling. Every time our hands came down, they touched, and then we both stopped and lay in the snow, arms and legs wide, holding hands in the middle.

I turned my head towards Liam at the same time he turned his head towards me. He had snow in his hair, his cheeks and nose were bright red, and his eyes sparkled with excitement.

'Why can't life always be like this?' he asked.

'Soggy feet, wet clothes, and numb cheeks?' I joked.

Liam smiled. 'Perhaps not that. I mean like this. Just the two of us together with nobody else in sight. No matter how bad things get, it's never really bad when it's us against the world.'

'Outcasts united,' I said.

'Outcasts united,' Liam agreed.

We lay in silence for a while, staring up at the snow-laden sky.

'What do you want, Carly?' Liam asked eventually.

'For Christmas?'

'No, not for Christmas.' He let go of my hand and propped himself up on his side to face me. 'If you could wish for anything right now, what would it be? And I don't mean something silly like having dry socks. I mean if you could have your heart's desire, what would you wish for?'

I shifted onto my side too. 'Why? Do you know what your heart's desire would be?'

'Yes. I've known for a while.'

'What is it?' I asked, intrigued.

He shook his head. 'I asked you first.'

As I gazed into his bright blue eyes, my tummy did a funny sort of cartwheel and I felt my heart race. I found myself staring at his lips and wondering what it would be like to kiss him. I'd never felt like that before. The feeling was strange, scary and quite exciting.

But we never got to share our heart's desires with each other because a snowball hit me square on the jaw. We'd both been oblivious to the Biscuit Bunch entering the field with a crowd of their male admirers and preparing their attack.

When we finally escaped from the onslaught, me with a cut on my cheek and Liam with a black eye thanks to the compacted ice balls the bullies had made, Liam received a call to say that his granddad had been rushed to hospital with a suspected heart attack. Sadly, he died the following morning and an appropriate moment never arose again to continue that conversation and I never thought consciously about kissing him again until that evening in The Old Theatre which Elodie also ruined.

Back in Castle Street, I turned my head towards the untouched snow to my left, stretching towards the road and Castle Park. It was begging for it.

'This is for you, Liam,' I said, lying down in the middle of the snow-covered cobbles and swishing my arms and legs. 'What's my heart's desire? It's you, of course.'

'That's very kind of you, love, but I'm already married.'

I sat upright, cringing, as the man in fluorescent work gear grinned and continued on his way.

'Sorry,' I called.

His laugh echoed back down the street.

Talking to my icing figures and propositioning strangers while creating snow angels in the middle of the street? I definitely, *definitely,* needed to get a life. I scrambled to my feet, shook off as much snow as I could, and unlocked the door to Carly's Cupcakes.

In fresh, dry clothes ten minutes later, I thought back to that day in the field with Liam. What had been his heart's desire? Could it have been me? My heart skipped a beat, but I dismissed the thought. It had probably been something like wanting to grow tall, to be accepted, or see the Biscuit Bunch have their come-uppance; the same stuff we usually talked about on our walks or bike rides. I frowned. No, it couldn't have been anything like that. He'd already shared all of that with me and his heart's desire was definitely something new he'd been about to reveal. Perhaps that could be my opener when ... if ... I dared to have the conversation about how I felt about him; a conversation I could have in three days' time. My heart raced at the thought of seeing him again, but my stomach churned at the thought of taking that scary leap of faith.

## 11

Shortly after 7.30 a.m., my mobile rang. My shoulders sagged as Bethany's name flashed on the screen. 'Don't you dare let me down today,' I muttered.

'Hi, Bethany.' I injected as much positivity in my tone as I could.

'It's actually Joshua,' he said. 'Sorry to confuse you.' I loved Joshua's voice – the gentle hint of a Scottish accent blended with North Yorkshire tones.

'Hi Joshua. Is everything okay?'

'No. Bethany's been throwing up all night.'

My stomach sank to the floor. 'Oh no! Something she ate?'

'I don't think so because we've had the same things and I'm fine. To be honest, I think it's the stress of everything that's happened with my parents and the wedding this week. I think it's taken its toll on her.'

He was probably right. Poor Bethany. 'How was it with your parents last night?'

'Awkward. A wee truce has been called but the damage has already been done. What my mum said was hurtful and completely uncalled for and, although Bethany was very gracious last night, I personally can't forgive and forget that quickly. She was inconsolable on Tuesday night. She even suggested calling off the wedding because she didn't want to come between me and my family.'

'She didn't mention that to me.'

Joshua sighed. 'Probably because I managed to talk her round. I love my parents but, if they were to make me choose, it would be Bethany every time.'

Tears pricked my eyes. How amazing must it be to have someone to love you so deeply that all they wanted was for it to be just you and them against the world? I thought about that day in the field again and the snow angels. That's what Liam had wanted; just the two of us.

'She's very lucky to have you,' I said. 'Is she asleep now?'

'Yes. She said to tell you she's really sorry about yesterday and even more sorry to be letting you down again today. She was feeling a wee bit better this morning but she knows she can't risk being round food in case it's really a stomach bug.'

'She's right. I need her to be clear for forty-eight hours before she can come back so I guess I'll see her back at work on Monday and at the dress-fitting in the meantime.'

'Sorry to be the bearer of bad news,' Joshua said. From the weariness in his voice, the stress had clearly got to him too.

'It's not your fault. These things happen. Send her my love.'

When I disconnected the call, I released a frustrated cry and stamped my feet. After everything that had happened that week, I wasn't surprised that Bethany was sick and I could well believe it was stress-related, but it left me completely stuffed. There was no way I could cope on my own for the next two days.

I picked up my phone and called Tara. 'I'm sorry to call you so early,' I said as soon as she answered. 'I've got an emergency.'

'You've grown a backbone and sacked your sister but you need some help in the shop?'

'Close. She's got a stomach bug so she won't be back till Monday and I'm way behind. Do you think any of your part-timers might be interested in working a shift for me today and tomorrow?'

'I'm sure I can find someone. Give me ten minutes to finish getting the scones in the oven then I'll make some calls. I'll ring you back within half an hour. Is that okay?'

'You're a lifesaver. If you can find me someone, we'll go out in the New Year and the drinks will be on me.'

Tara laughed. 'Never work with family and never offer to pay for drinks all night for someone who can drink like a fish when she's in the mood. I'll call you later.'

I watched with admiration as one of Tara's part-time students, seventeen-year-old Lana, swiftly packaged up half a dozen cupcakes while effortlessly chatting to the customer. I owed Tara big time. Most of her team were keen to work extra shifts so she'd juggled things round for me.

'Are you okay if I leave you to it?' I asked after I'd shown Lana where to find the various boxes and bags.

Lana smiled. 'No problem. The till's simpler than next door's and the offers are on the blackboard so I'm good, thanks. You're only out the back if I need you?'

'Yes. I'll be in my workshop which, right now, resembles Santa's workshop. If you get anyone wanting to place an order or collect anything, give me a shout. If the phone rings, I'll pick it up so no need to worry about that either.'

'Okay. I'll familiarise myself with your products first. Tara likes us to know exactly what's available.'

I smiled at her. 'Wow! She's taught you well. If you're going to familiarise yourself with my products, the best way is to try them. Do you like cake?'

She grinned and rubbed her flat stomach. 'I live for cake.'

I reached into the display counter and lifted out two of the more basic cupcakes. 'Here, try these. Can you remember which is which flavour just by looking at the wrappers?'

Lana nodded. 'Red wrappers are vanilla sponge and green wrappers are chocolate.'

'Perfect. I'll leave you to it.'

* * *

Lana was a delight to have around. She was very confident with customers, talking them into purchasing more cupcakes than they'd originally asked for, or more intricate costlier designs. As I listened, it struck me that my plan to build Bethany up had been short-lived. She'd dismissed the positive comments about her sales techniques and I'd got so bogged down with my work that I hadn't continued to give her compliments.

'What are you making?' Lana asked, appearing in the archway when there was a lull in the shop around mid-morning. 'It smells delicious in here.'

'One hundred vanilla cupcakes,' I said, continuing to place them one by one onto cooling racks. 'I'll be decorating them as snowmen, polar bears and Christmas trees later.'

'Are they for the shop?'

'No. The mayor's hosting a party at The Ramparts Hotel tomorrow afternoon for disadvantaged kids. Several local businesses get involved and give their products or services at a discount. I heard about it through Tara a few years back.'

Lana gasped. 'A hundred cupcakes? That's loads. What sort of discount do you give?'

I laughed. I liked Lana's confidence and could see why she got on so well with Tara because she had the same tell-it-like-it-is no-nonsense approach. 'Actually, I do them for free.'

'That's very generous.'

'It's for a good cause so I'm happy to help and I usually get the investment back, although that's not why I do it. The hotel produces a leaflet thanking all the contributors which acts like an advertising flier. Guests can pick it up in the lobby and the mayor emails a copy to his huge network of contacts and I always get business from that.'

'How do you know?'

I smiled at her curiosity. 'I include a promotional code which is unique to each piece of advertising so I know what does and doesn't work.' I'd actually had a few enquiries today, all quoting the same code. I couldn't place where it had come from but would check later. 'I also give out an envelope of business cards with each cake collection and ask customers if they'll leave them out at their event. They have unique codes too.'

'Very clever,' Lana said.

'Thank you but I can't take the credit for it. It was my sister's suggestion when I first set up the shop.' I frowned. Until I'd said it aloud just then, I'd forgotten it had been Bethany's idea. Something else I had to praise Bethany for when I saw her. She was really good at the sales and marketing stuff. Maybe I could task her with coming up with new marketing ideas. If she could generate extra business, I could afford to keep her on *and* pay for someone to help me with the cakes. Could that be the way forward?

The sound of a customer arriving pulled Lana back into the shop.

I began rolling out the white icing for the polar bears, wondering whether there were any other suggestions that Bethany had made that had proved valuable. Even though she was prone to being overly dramatic when disaster struck, she tended to be very subtle when it came to putting forward ideas. There'd been no big build-up when she'd come up with the code idea – just a subtle suggestion – and she'd been the one who'd suggested having different colour wrappers on the cupcakes to easily distinguish between sponge flavours. So simple yet so effective.

During my first year of trading, she'd decided hairdressing wasn't for her and had taken a part-time job as a dog groomer. With time off during the week, she'd often pop in for a chat and had suggested I create a samples box for wedding organisers and party planners in the area. She'd then driven round distributing them for me. I'd had loads of business on the back of that and was now the cake decorator most of them recommended to their clients as a result. Of course, I'd thanked her at the time but she'd refused to take any credit, saying I'd have thought of it myself eventually. She might have cost me some money recently but that was peanuts compared to the money she'd made for the business. Maybe she wasn't such a liability after all.

## 12

'Morning,' Lana said, arriving at the shop on Saturday morning. 'How's your sister?'

'Much better, thanks. She hasn't been sick again so she'll be fine to return on Monday.' I'd called Bethany last night but had only managed to speak to Joshua who said she was in the bath and planning on an early night afterwards.

Having seen my sister nearly every day since she'd started working in the shop, I felt at a bit of a loss without the regular contact. Despite the mishaps, I missed her singing and her bubbly personality. It was a little too quiet without her.

'That's good news,' Lana said, removing her coat and hanging it up.

'Do you know what shifts you're working next week?' I asked.

Lana nodded. 'Tuesday and Friday all day, plus Wednesday afternoon.'

'In that case, would you like to work here on the days you're not next door? Even with Bethany back, I could use the extra pair of hands. We're closed on Friday for the wedding but I can make use of you the days you're not working and also next Saturday if Tara doesn't need you.'

Lana beamed. 'Really? That would be amazing.'

'I'll ring Tara later and check it's okay with her.'

'Thank you.' Lana filled the kettle and put it on to boil. 'What are you making today?'

'I'm finishing off a twenty-first birthday cake for collection at four, then working on another Christmas one.'

'Is this the twenty-first cake?' she asked, wandering over to the table. I'd already iced it, the bottom tier with deep purple icing and the top tier with white.

'Yes. I need to put some coloured stripes on the top tier and a pattern on the bottom.' I lifted up a small plastic cocktail glass. 'This will sit on the top and there'll be a woman lying in the glass holding a drink which will have stars exploding out of it.'

'You're so creative. I can't wait to see it finished.'

The kettle clicked off so Lana set about making the drinks. She handed me a coffee a couple of minutes later. 'I loved the cake you made for my cousin's christening. It was simple but beautiful.'

'Which one was that?' I asked, rolling out some lilac icing ready for the stripes.

'Baby Thea last Sunday.'

My stomach lurched and I spun round to face Lana. 'Thea Hargreaves?'

'That's right.'

'Jasper Hargreaves is your uncle?'

Lana nodded. 'Auntie Andrea – Jasper's wife – is my dad's sister.'

'Small world,' I muttered as I returned to rolling the icing.

'I don't really like Uncle Jasper,' Lana continued. 'Especially after what he said about you. There's no way you'd ever let anyone down and it wasn't fair of him to suggest you had.'

'What do you mean?' I snapped my head up and twisted round again.

'Auntie Andrea was really annoyed with him for not picking up the cake until the morning of the christening and they had a fight about it. He told her you'd forgotten to do it which was why it was last minute and not the design she wanted but, at the christening, I overheard him telling one of his friends that he'd forgotten to order it and had sweet-talked his ex-girlfriend into pulling an all-nighter to make it for him.' She wrinkled her nose in apparent disgust. 'Did you really go out with Uncle Jasper?'

I stared at Lana, barely registering the last question. 'Let me get this right. Jasper forgot to order the cake in the first place?'

'That's right.'

'Somebody else didn't let him down before he came to me?'

'No. He forgot.'

'The devious little…' I only just managed to stop myself from swearing in front of Lana.

'He told his friend you still love him and that's why you made the cake,' Lana said. 'You don't, do you?'

'I most certainly do not. How dare he?'

Lana wrinkled her nose again. 'Sorry. Should I have kept quiet? Tara always tells me to say what's on my mind, but I don't think everyone always likes to hear it.'

I took a deep calming breath and smiled at her. 'It's fine. I'm glad I know.'

The bell tinkled. 'I'll leave you to it,' Lana said, heading into the shop.

Resuming my rolling – perhaps a bit too aggressively – I muttered expletives under my breath. I'd get him back. I wasn't sure how, but I'd definitely get him back for that. I would stop at nothing to protect the reputation of the business. How dare he spread lies like that?

* * *

'Only me,' Bethany called as she arrived at the shop shortly after 4.30 p.m., just missing Lana.

I put down the snowman I was moulding and headed into the shop, arms wide.

'Are you okay?' I asked, hugging her.

'I'm sorry I let you down.'

'It's not your fault. If you're sick, you're sick, and I can't let you near food so you did the right thing to stay away.'

Bethany pulled away. 'I mean on Thursday. I shouldn't have stormed out like that. It was a massive over-reaction and I'm sorry. I don't know what's up with me at the moment. I feel like such a drama queen now.'

I shook my head. 'Forget it, but don't do it again.'

'I won't, but that's because I won't be working here. I'm handing in my notice.'

They were the words I'd thought so many times that I wanted to hear but now that she was saying them, they filled me with dread instead of relief. 'Bethany! No!'

She gave me a weak smile. 'My mind's made up. You've given me more than enough chances and I've messed up each time. I'll work on Monday through to Wednesday next week if you still want me but I'll be out of your hair after that.' She released what sounded like a nervous laugh. 'You're now free to look for someone who can actually use a piping bag to decorate the cakes instead of the walls.'

Even though she was smiling at me and cracking a joke, I could hear the wobble in her voice. I could hear the doubt. 'You really don't have to leave,' I said gently.

She looked at me with sad eyes and shook her head slowly. 'You and I both know that I do,' she said in a soft voice. 'I've outstayed my welcome but it's been fun. I've enjoyed working with my big sister.'

'And I've loved having you here, despite the occasional mishap.'

'Occasional?' Bethany raised her eyebrows. 'Every day, you mean.'

I wanted to remind her of all the great ideas she'd come up with and how much money she'd made for the business but I was on a deadline, as always, and I wanted to do it properly over drinks or a meal.

'Yes please to working next week,' I said. 'And I'm not accepting your notice. Not so close to Christmas.'

'You don't have a choice.'

I didn't have time to argue. 'Are you okay to mind the shop for the last half an hour while I crack on? I think you're probably safe to be round food now.'

Bethany removed her hat, scarf and coat and handed them to me. 'It's the least I can do.'

\* \* \*

'I'm gutted that the snow's gone already,' Bethany said as I locked up the shop forty minutes later. 'I love first-footing but I slept through most of it and missed out. I hope we get some more.'

'Do you know what I did yesterday morning?' I asked, linking her arm as we headed a couple of doors up the street to The Wedding Emporium on the other side of The Chocolate Pot. I was friends with the owner, Ginny, and she'd offered to stay open later so that I didn't have to close early for my dress fitting.

'No idea,' Bethany said. 'What did you do?'

'I ran up and down Castle Street, first-footing on each side of the street, and then I made a snow angel outside the shop.'

'You didn't!'

'I did.'

'I bet everyone thought you were mad.'

'It was early so there was no one around when I ran up and down the street although I did get seen doing my snow angel and that was embarrassing.' I decided not to share the conversation about my heart's desire.

We knocked on the door to The Wedding Emporium.

'Good evening, ladies,' Ginny said, beaming at us. 'I've been looking forward to this all day. Your dresses are absolutely stunning.'

She closed the door behind us and locked it, then she and I put our hands over our ears as squeals filled the air while Bethany hugged her four best friends.

When they'd calmed down, Ginny handed us each a glass of bubbly. 'Bride first?' she asked.

Everyone enthusiastically agreed so Ginny disappeared with Bethany. Amanda, Robyn and Leyla asked me about my day and cooed about the cakes displayed in my window but Paige simply glowered at me.

'I'm ready,' Bethany called from the other side of the curtains. 'You've got to imagine this with my hair up and my make-up done properly, but here we go.' Ginny pulled the curtain back and tears rushed to my eyes. I hadn't seen the dress or even a picture of it because Bethany had wanted to go dress-hunting with Mum and they'd both kept it strictly secret. It was gorgeous. In a warm cream, the V-necked bodice and straps were covered in lace flowers and iridescent sparkles. The same pattern decorated the base of the full skirt and a band of silver sparkles round the waist finished the dress off perfectly.

'It's got a small train,' Bethany said, twisting round so we could see. 'What do you think?'

'You look so beautiful,' I said, swallowing the lump in my throat.

Bethany stayed in her dress for the next ten minutes or so, swishing it and showing us how it would look with her cream faux fur trimmed cape. Amanda, Robyn and Leyla fussed round her, pulling out the train and arranging the folds of the cape, gushing about how gorgeous she looked. Paige stayed in her seat, steadily topping up her glass until the bottle was empty.

'What do you think, Paige?' Bethany asked.

'A bit fussy for my taste, but it suits you.' Paige raised her glass as a toast.

'Aw, thanks, Paige. I'm so glad you like it.'

I clenched my teeth. There she was again, having a little dig, yet nobody seemed to notice. Watching Paige curl her lip as she looked Bethany up and down, I suspected that she hated my sister being centre stage instead of her.

'Enough about me,' Bethany said. 'I'll get Ginny to help me out of this, then I'm beyond excited about seeing you all in your dresses. I've had a sneak preview and they're so beautiful.'

'Right,' Ginny said, when Bethany was back in her jeans and T-shirt. 'One at a time or all together?'

'All together,' Bethany's friends chorused.

'So, what have we got here?' Ginny said, reaching round the curtain. 'Spaghetti straps which I believe is for Robyn.'

Robyn squealed and grabbed the dress, stroking the fabric.

'A one-shoulder design for Amanda,' Ginny continued. 'Lacy back and sleeves for you, Carly.' She handed out the two dresses. 'Which just leaves the strapless and V-neck ones. Here we go. V-neck for Leyla and strapless for Paige.' She held the two dresses up.

'Other way round,' Leyla said, giggling.

I caught Ginny's shocked expression. 'Erm, I don't think that's right.' Ginny looked towards Bethany for help. 'The, erm, the V-neck is... erm... the smallest dress I was asked to order and the strapless one is the larger of the sizes.'

There was an awkward silence.

'Are you saying the V-neck dress is the size eight?' Leyla asked.

Ginny nodded, still holding up a dress in each hand.

Leyla shrugged and smiled. 'Okay. I don't mind. They're both really pretty. I can wear this one.' She reached for the V-neck.

'So I have to wear this one?' Paige leapt to her feet, grabbed the strapless one and waved it in the air. 'Hello? A strapless dress with these boobs and these arms? This is a wind-up, right?'

I glanced at Bethany who had her hand over her mouth and was looking distinctly pale.

'I don't think anyone's winding anyone up, Paige,' I said. 'It looks like those two dresses might have been ordered in the wrong sizes but why don't you try the strapless one on? I think you'll look fabulous in it.'

'They look great on a fuller figure,' Ginny assured her. 'You might be surprised at how sturdy the bodice is.'

'I'm not trying it on,' Paige snapped. 'I'm not having you all laughing at me when my boobs fall out.'

'We wouldn't laugh,' Amanda said. 'Please try it on, Paige.'

Paige gave her a filthy look then turned and pointed at Bethany. 'You did this deliberately, didn't you?'

'No. It was an accident. I'm so sorry, Paige.'

'Accident, my arse. You've been waiting all year for your revenge. This is you getting back at me for what happened with Joshua at New Year, isn't it?'

'What happened at New Year?' Bethany asked, her voice shaking.

Paige planted her hands on her hips. 'Don't play Little Miss Innocent with me. I *know* he told you.'

Bethany took a step closer to her and managed to inject some strength in her voice. 'What did you do? Did you try it on with him?'

Paige shrugged. 'I was drunk.'

'You were drunk? You were *drunk*? And that gives you the right to throw yourself at somebody else's fiancé?'

'I didn't know he was going to propose,' Paige cried. 'I thought he was just your boyfriend.'

A collective gasp went round the room.

'What are you lot gasping at?' Paige rounded on the others. 'How was I supposed to know he was going to propose at midnight?'

'Oh my God, Paige!' Bethany cried. 'Being *just* my boyfriend didn't signal to you that he was off limits?'

'No, because I didn't think it would last.' She turned to Bethany. 'You've always been so flaky, in and out of love and in and out of jobs. I thought that Joshua would end up being another of your pretty-boy cast-offs and I thought he could do better.'

'And that meant being with you?'

'Yes! He's too good for you. Can't you see that?'

They'd both gradually moved closer to each other as the other girls looked on in shock. Any moment, it could end in one of them throwing a punch. I jumped to my feet and put my arm protectively round my sister, gently pulling her away from Paige. 'I think you should probably go home, Paige. You clearly have some serious jealousy issues that you need to resolve and you—'

'Jealousy issues? Of her? The girl who can't even hold down a job with her own sister? The girl whose in-laws don't want her to marry their son?'

I could feel Bethany trembling next to me and I tightened my grip, pulling her close to my side. 'Out. Now.'

'Don't worry, I'm going. Any of you lot coming?' She turned and faced the other three. Amanda and Robyn were holding hands and silently sobbing. Leyla kept opening and closing her mouth like a fish, eyes wide with shock. 'Didn't think so. Thanks a lot for the support just now. Great friends you turned out to be.' She pulled on her coat. 'See you around.'

She marched towards the door but Leyla leapt to her feet and grabbed Paige's arm. 'What were you thinking, making a move on Joshua? It would have made no difference if Bethany and Joshua had been married or if they'd just met. He was off limits. Friends don't do that to each other.'

Paige shrugged her off. 'Friends? Don't make me laugh. It was always the four of you, looking down your noses at me, desperate for an excuse to get rid of me. Well, now you've got your excuse. Well done. The fat lass has been ditched.'

'It was never like that,' Amanda cried. 'You were *always* one of us.'

'Oh, get over yourself.' Paige grabbed for the door handle but Ginny had locked it when Bethany and I arrived. 'Let me out,' she shouted, rattling the door.

A relieved-looking Ginny headed towards the door with a set of keys but Bethany put out her hand to stop her and took a couple of steps towards Paige.

'I don't know what happened tonight or why it happened, but I'm glad it did because I don't want to be sharing my wedding day with someone who clearly hates me and wants to destroy my relationship. I've never treated you with anything but love and kindness. I didn't deliberately mess up your bridesmaid dress order. Why would I do something like that? It was a genuine mistake. You making a move on Joshua, drunk or not, was *not* a mistake. That was deliberate and that was unforgivable.' She turned to Ginny. 'You can let her out now, thank you. At least we've solved one problem. She won't have to wear that strapless bridesmaid dress because she won't be at my wedding.'

When Ginny locked the door behind Paige, Bethany crumpled onto the chair that Paige had vacated. Her friends gathered round her, hugging her and whispering reassurances. I have no idea where she found the strength to make that confident speech but I had to give her massive respect for managing to hold it together like that.

Leaving the girls to have a bonding moment, I made my way over to Ginny who was still standing by the door looking shell-shocked. 'I'm guessing that was probably a first for a dress-fitting.'

Ginny widened her eyes. 'Thankfully, yes. Will she be all right?' She nodded towards Bethany.

'I'm not sure. I hope so but she's had a shocker of a week.' I shook my head in disbelief. It turned out I'd been right to dislike Paige, but I could never in a million years have predicted that outburst. Bethany didn't need someone like that in her life, and neither did the other girls.

Trying the bridesmaid dresses on after the incident with Paige had lost its sparkle but still had to be done. Ginny and I did our best to lighten the atmosphere, but it wasn't going to be easy for any of them to get over it.

'Would you mind if we skipped drinks?' Bethany asked the others. 'I want to get back to Joshua and find out exactly what happened at New Year.'

'He won't have done anything,' Amanda said.

'No, he'll have pushed her off,' Leyla agreed.

Bethany gave them a weak smile. 'I know and, to be fair to her, Paige suggested it was one-sided, but I want to hear it from him and understand why he never said anything to me, particularly if he told her that he was going to.'

'He probably didn't want to cause friction between you and Paige,' Robyn suggested.

Bethany nodded. 'That sounds very like Joshua but, even so, I want to chat to him about it. You do understand, don't you?'

They all said they did and wished her luck.

'Before we say goodnight, does anyone have anything else they want to confess?' Bethany asked. 'Nobody else tried to play tonsil hockey with my fiancé? No? That's a relief.'

\* \* \*

Back in my workshop, I found it really hard to concentrate. I kept replaying the altercation with Paige. She clearly had some serious issues with all of them and I wondered whether I should have said something to Bethany when I'd noticed all of Paige's snide remarks. Would it have made any difference? Would it have stopped tonight's incident? Probably not.

I cast my mind back to Bethany's childhood when Paige had frequently played at our house, stayed for dinner and had sleepovers. She'd been loud and bossy but had she been nasty back then or had that kicked in when the pair became a group at senior school?

With a sigh, I put my tools down, made my way up to the flat and dug out a plastic crate from under my bed containing photos and memorabilia. I lifted out theatre programmes, cards and postcards to reveal a stack of photos in envelopes. I rummaged through them until I found snaps I'd taken at Bethany's eighth birthday party. All the photos of her and Paige together showed two young friends laughing. Several more envelopes revealed more of the same. I'm not sure what I'd expected to find. Paige standing in the background giving my sister filthy looks? Paige pulling Bethany's hair or digging her nails into her arm? Nothing.

'Well, that was a pointless waste of time,' I muttered, sighing as I shoved everything higgledy-piggledy back in the crate. I was about to replace the lid when something caught my eye. A homemade card. Frowning, I lifted it out and studied the beautiful drawings and accompanying words on both the outside and inside.

'Oh my goodness,' I whispered, leaning back against the bed. 'The shop was Bethany's idea.'

The day Mrs Armstrong announced The Cake Shop was closing, I was distraught. She gave me a hug and sent me home early telling me not to worry and everything would work out for the best. How could it? I loved my job. I'd have happily done it forever.

As soon as I got home, I phoned Jasper but he was no comfort. 'Why are you getting upset?' he said. 'It's *only* a job.'

Mum and Dad had gone away for a week to celebrate their thirtieth wedding anniversary and, much as I'd have loved their counsel, I didn't want to put a dampener on their holiday.

Bethany was nineteen at the time and working in a hairdressing salon. When she arrived home, I was still in bits. She hugged me and asked what was wrong.

'That's rubbish,' she said after I'd told her my news. 'But you'll soon find another job, won't you?'

I smiled at her positivity. 'Probably, but The Cake Shop is the only cake decorating shop in town so I won't find another job the same. I love it there so much. I can't bear the thought of it ending.'

'You're lucky,' Bethany said. 'I hate my job. All I seem to do all day is make coffee and sweep up hair. What is it that you love about your job?'

'Everything. There isn't one part of it that I don't love.'

'What do you love most, then?' she asked.

I thought for a moment. 'The look on a customer's face when I've brought their vision to life. I don't think I'll ever tire of that.' I smiled at her. 'When they let you start cutting hair and you get to transform how a customer looks, you'll get that same feeling.'

She shrugged. 'Maybe. Good luck with the job hunting. I'm sure you'll find something really soon.'

I hadn't expected Bethany to understand. She'd only been working for ten months, was already at her second salon, and it was fairly obvious that she was regretting her career choice. Loving your job was clearly an alien concept to her. I had expected Jasper to have been more sympathetic, though. I longed to speak to Liam who'd definitely get it but he was away on an oilrig on some work training thing so non-contactable.

At about 10.00 p.m. that evening, there'd been a knock on my bedroom door and Bethany poked her head round it.

'I made you this.' She closed the door, sat beside me on my bed, and handed me a homemade card.

I looked down at the drawing of The Cake Shop on the front with a big SOLD sign across the closed front door. 'It's a good likeness,' I said.

'Thank you.'

'"When one door closes..."' I read, before opening the card, '"... another one opens".' Inside, there was a drawing of a different cake shop with an open door. The sign above it read 'Carly's Cupcakes.'

Bethany gently nudged me. 'What do you think?'

'I think you should probably have studied art. You're really good at drawing.'

She didn't respond – just stared at the card in my hands – then stood up. 'Night, Carly.'

'Night, Bethany. Thanks for this.' I stood the card on my bedside drawers. 'It's lovely.'

She hovered in the doorway as though she wanted to say something else. I looked up at her expectantly but she shrugged and closed the door behind her.

A couple of days later, I was in denial about The Cake Shop closing. I kept hoping that Mrs Armstrong would have a last minute change of heart or the estate agent would pull out of the purchase. I imagined the shop being sold instead and me being able to work for the new owner.

'This *is* happening, you know, my dear,' Mrs Armstrong said, as

I helped her re-price the stock for the closing-down sale. 'The shop *is* closing.'

I couldn't bring myself to respond.

'The paperwork has been signed and I've booked a long overdue cruise. On 31ˢᵗ July, we close the doors for good.'

'But you love this place. You love making cakes. What will you do without it?'

'Oh, Carly, I *do* love this place and I'm sure I'll shed a tear on my last day, but The Cake Shop isn't my *whole* life. It's simply *part* of my life. It's time for the next part to start now. Mr Armstrong's retiring too and we're looking forward to some quality time together. We want to travel, work on the garden, and see more of our grand-children.'

My shoulders slumped. 'I don't know what I'm going to do. I saw Jasper last night and he didn't get it. He said that, if I love decorating cakes that much, I should do it from home.'

'It's a possibility,' Mrs Armstrong said.

I shook my head. 'It's an *im*possibility. Mum and Dad's kitchen isn't very big and it wouldn't be fair of me to take it over even if it was suitable. I can't turn their home into my business and I can't afford to move out and kit out my own home with a decent kitchen. Besides, I like the set-up of the shop.'

'I understand, lovey. Doing this from home isn't for everyone. It never appealed to me.'

The following day, I helped her take an inventory of the equipment. She looked through the bookings diary and shook her head. 'I'm not looking forward to letting all these customers down.'

'How many bookings are there?'

She sighed as she flicked back and forth through the pages. 'Thirty? Forty? Maybe even fifty?' She closed the book. 'If you were to set up at home, lovey, you wouldn't have to start from scratch. You'd already have a portfolio of customers right here.'

She tapped the cover of the diary before placing it on the counter.

I wasn't sure how to respond. Doing it from home simply wasn't an option.

She opened the kitchen door and whistled. 'Look at all that equipment. So many quality pieces, lots of it new. It would be perfect for someone looking to set up their own business, don't you think?'

I joined her in the doorway and nodded. 'It certainly would be.'

'So do you want it?'

I frowned at her. 'Me? As I said yesterday, being based from home isn't an option.'

'Agreed. But you could always set up your own cake shop.'

My jaw dropped. 'Are you being serious?'

She smiled widely. 'You've got the talent, the customer service and the business sense so all you need is the equipment, customers and premises. I can't help you with the premises, but I *can* help you with the equipment and the customers.'

I turned and looked round the shop, my eyes resting on the bookings' diary on the counter. 'It would be an amazing starter pack for someone.'

'It would be an amazing starter pack for *you*.'

Excitement bubbled inside me. My own shop? But then reality hit and I shook my head. 'Even if I could find suitable premises and afford to kit it out, there's no way I could afford to buy the equipment too.'

Mrs Armstrong patted my arm gently. 'Did I say anything about payment, lovey? I was thinking we could call it your redundancy package. I won't get much for it if I try to sell it and I'd rather it goes to a good home.'

My jaw dropped open. Had I heard her right?

'Why don't you look online tonight and see if there are any

premises available and we'll talk some more tomorrow? But I mean it, the equipment would be your redundancy and the order book would be a thank you for years of loyalty. Most of the customers in there are regulars and you decorate their cakes anyway so nothing would change for them except the shop location.'

I rushed home from work that day, full of excitement, and grabbed my laptop, searching for retail premises in Whitsborough Bay.

'What are you doing?' Bethany asked when she arrived home from the salon.

'Looking for shops in town.'

'For your own cake shop?' She threw herself down on the sofa beside me and looked at the screen.

'I like the look of this one,' I said, clicking onto the details of an empty premises on Castle Street. I recognised it as a gift shop that had closed earlier in the year. 'I'm going to see if I can get an appointment to look round it at the weekend when Mum and Dad are back. I'll need to look into a business loan too. I daren't get too excited yet because I might not be able to make it happen.'

'I'm so glad you're looking into it,' Bethany said. 'When one door closes, another one opens and this one will be to your very own cake shop.'

I never made the connection at the time. Not once, at any point during the months that followed in which I secured funding and prepared the shop, did Bethany claim credit for the idea or the business name, but she'd definitely been there first. She'd planted the seed of an idea on that card and I'd never realised. Until now.

# 13

As I worked on Sunday morning, I kept glancing at the clock, wondering how early it would be acceptable to call Bethany to ask how it had gone with Joshua last night. I'd really struggled to sleep, replaying the ugly scenes with Paige in my mind and worrying about how this was going to affect my sister. At 7.30 a.m., I sent Bethany a text, asking her to call as soon as she was able. When Bethany's name flashed up with a FaceTime request shortly after eight, I grabbed the phone, not caring that I was getting icing on it.

'Bethany! Are you okay? How's Joshua?'

'We're both fine.' Her voice sounded strained and she wasn't smiling so I was relieved when she added, 'There's still going to be a wedding.'

'So what happened at New Year?' I asked.

'Nothing much.' She shook her head. 'I don't know if you remember but we went to a party on a farm up the coast. Joshua says Paige was touchy-feely with him all night. He didn't think much of it at first because she's always like that, especially when she's been drinking, but it got worse as the night went on. A bit of flirting turned to some suggestive remarks and he didn't know what to do. He asked her to tone it down but she kept saying that she loved it when men played hard to get.'

'What was she playing at?' I said. 'I can't believe someone would do that to their best friend's boyfriend. I wouldn't dream of it.'

'Neither would I, but that's because we have morals. Some people, like Paige, obviously don't.' She grimaced and I could tell from her expression that she was still hurting. 'Anyway, Joshua didn't want to cause friction between Paige and me by making an issue of it so he ended up spending the evening trying to avoid her. I can remember him disappearing a lot that night and now it makes sense.

'It was really loud and hot in the barn so Joshua got a drink and took it outside but Paige followed him. He turned to head back to the barn but she stopped him and said that there was no need to leave because of her, apologised for flirting and said she hadn't meant to make him uncomfortable. Then she suddenly burst into tears so Joshua did exactly what I'd expect him to do with any of my friends if they were upset. He gave her a hug and told her it would all be all right. Next thing he knows, she's trying to ram her tongue down his throat.' She stuck her tongue out and grimaced. 'He pushed her off but she kept lunging at him, saying that it could be their little secret and I didn't need to know. He told her he had no secrets from me and would be telling me exactly what she'd done. He stormed back into the barn to find me.'

'Why didn't he tell you?'

'I was on the dance floor with Amanda, Robyn and Leyla. We had our arms round each other and were in fits of giggles about something. Watching us, it struck him how important my friends were to me and how devastated I'd be to lose any of them. He figured he could either tell me about Paige and change our friendship forever or put it down to a moment of drunken stupidity on Paige's part. Plus, he was planning to propose at midnight so it really wasn't a good time to risk upsetting me. It's typical Joshua, looking out for me all the time.' For the first time in the call, she smiled as she spoke tenderly about him.

'That makes sense.' I sighed. 'Have you heard from Paige?'

'No, and I don't think I will. She's ditched us all on social media.'

'Her loss, not yours.'

'I know, but it's such a shock to have one of your closest friends turn on you like that.'

'Paige isn't the sort of person that any of you need in your life so please promise me you won't waste any more energy thinking about her. The other three are lovely. Focus on them instead, and on Joshua.'

'I will,' she said in a small voice, making my heart ache for her.

'Are you going to be okay?' I asked, looking at her image earnestly.

'I'm fine. Honestly. It's just a lot to process.'

'Your other friends are lovely,' I reassured her. 'They've got your back.'

She smiled. 'I know. Thank you. I'll let you get back to work and I'll see you tomorrow.'

We said goodbye and I put my phone down. She'd been best friends with Paige since the age of six so that betrayal will have hurt her badly, especially when she was already feeling bruised about being a failure. I might not have had many friends over the years, but at least I'd never experienced anything like that. There was a lot to be said for having one constant best friend and it only ever being the two of us. Mind you, my friendship with Liam came with different complications.

\* \* \*

By 5.30 p.m., I was exhausted. Hunched up over the table all day with only a packet soup for lunch was not ideal but at least I'd finally caught up from the delays caused by squeezing in the christening cake for Jasper and from Bethany walking out.

Several of the Castle Street businesses were open on a Sunday but I'd resisted it knowing I'd burn out if I opened seven days a week, although it was very rare I actually got any time off. Those who opened on Sunday tended to close at 4.00 p.m. which meant that there wouldn't be many people around just now – perfect for a quick stroll and my first fresh air of the day before moving onto my next cake.

As I stepped out of the front door, I inhaled the delicious aroma of chimney smoke. I loved that smell. There was something about real fires that was so intrinsically Christmassy. I paused for a moment to look up at the white lights strung between the shops, like stars in the inky sky. It was the beautiful simplicity that made them so enchanting to look at.

Something wet landed on my nose, then on my cheek. I looked up at the sky again. More snow. Yes! Even more perfect for an evening stroll.

I thrust my gloved hands in my pockets as I meandered up Castle Street, looking at the Christmassy windows.

The Wedding Emporium's window display, which I'd barely glanced at last night, was stunning and so perfect for the season – a red and white wedding gown, a red adult bridesmaid dress, and a red and white child's dress. It looked as though snow was resting on the shoulders of the mannequins and on the floor, and there were deep red roses strewn across the floor too, among sprigs of holly.

The window of Bay Books depicted Santa's workshop. The elves were supposed to be busy making toys but were actually engrossed in reading books instead, resulting in toys tumbling off the conveyor belt.

I continued to move from window to window, smiling at each festive display and marvelling at how creative some of them were.

Near the end of Castle Street, opposite Seaside Blooms, I found my favourite. Bear With Me, a specialist teddy bear retailer, had a double frontage like many of the shops in the street. In one of the windows, there was a fireside scene. Santa's boots dangled above a tissue paper fire and cute plush teddy bears poked their heads out of colourful stockings hanging along the mantlepiece. In the other window, a beautifully-painted wooden sleigh was filled with more traditional-looking jointed teddies in various colours and sizes. Some were dressed in full winter finery, some in hats and scarves, and others were taking a chance that their fur would keep them warm enough.

Bethany, a huge fan of teddy bears, would have loved it. I'd never really been into them but, looking into their cute faces just now, I could see the appeal. With the snow round me fluttering to the ground, they suddenly seemed quite magical.

The ringing of my mobile tore my eyes away from the shop window. My heart leapt at Liam's name as I accepted the FaceTime call.

'You're not home early, are you?'

'I wish! The flight time's changed and I won't be back home until really late tomorrow night or maybe even the early hours of Tuesday. Are you free on Tuesday night to go out for a meal?'

I grinned. 'I might be able to shuffle a few things around in my incredibly hectic social schedule, just for you. Why don't you stop by the shop during the day, though?'

'Because it's your busiest time of year and you won't get any work done if I'm there to distract you.' He smiled so tenderly that my heart melted. 'I'm dying to see you but it will have to wait until your icing snowmen and Santas aren't vying for my attention.'

'Fair point,' I said. 'All good things come to those who wait. What time on Tuesday?'

'Seven?'

'Perfect. Have a safe journey home and wrap up warm because it's snowing in Whitsborough Bay.'

'Really? Right now?'

'Right now, although it's only just started.'

'Show me.'

I slowly turned in a circle, pointing the phone towards the sky then up and down the street before turning it back to me.

'I'm so jealous,' Liam said. 'I'd trade the heat of Afghanistan for snow any day. Do me a favour and take a selfie of you with some snow and send me it so I can pretend I'm there.'

'I wish you were here right now,' I said, feeling brave.

'So do I.' Liam's voice softened. 'I've missed you, Carls. I... Hang on...'

He turned his face to one side and I could hear him having a muffled conversation with someone before he turned back to face me.

'I've got to go,' he said. 'I'll be waiting for that photo.'

When he'd hung up, I checked myself in the selfie setting. There was colour in my cheeks and the snow had made my eyes sparkle. Snowflakes had settled on my hat and scarf, and in my long hair. Very wintery. Liam would approve.

Holding my phone out, I twisted position until I had the best angle of Castle Street, showing the most snow, then clicked and sent him the image.

Moments later, Liam responded with 'Beautiful xx'. My stomach did a somersault. *Does he mean me or Castle Street in the snow? Please let it be me!*

I put my phone in my pocket and turned to take one last look in the window of Bear With Me. 'Do you dare me to be brave and tell him how I feel?' I asked the bears.

'If you listen really carefully, they sometimes answer.'

I spun round and came face to face with the shop manager.

'Jemma! You scared the life out of me.'

'Sorry,' she said, smiling at me. 'I didn't mean to creep up on you like that. I got partway back to the car and realised I'd left my phone under the counter.' She pulled out her keys and unlocked the door. 'I have no idea who you were talking about but, unless he's married or underage, my advice would be to tell him.'

'You think so?'

She nodded. 'Definitely, and I speak from personal experience. It can be scary but sometimes you have to put yourself out there because the reward can be really worthwhile. Feel free to ask the bears for your heart's desire. Just make sure you listen to their answer although you might need to come into the shop to hear what they say. The glass is a bit thick for them.' Jemma winked then closed the door behind her leaving me laughing. To an outsider, they'd probably think that Jemma was a crazy-bearlady. I didn't know her well but I'd met her enough times to know it was tongue-in-cheek.

Although Jemma hadn't been making a dig, it struck me that the one and only time I'd been in Bear With Me was when I'd been about to open Carly's Cupcakes and had distributed my business cards. I'd dismissed the shop as something I wasn't into, yet I'd been captivated by those little faces in the window just now. Perhaps I needed to open my eyes a bit more. Maybe I'd take a rare break tomorrow and have a look round.

I took one last look at the bears then ambled back to my little corner of the world, thinking about Liam. In just over forty-eight hours, I'd be seeing him again and my life could change forever from that night.

# 14

ONE WEEK UNTIL CHRISTMAS

Shortly after 5.30 a.m. the following morning, I opened the lounge blinds in my flat and looked out over Castle Street. It had snowed heavily overnight, covering the street with a deep white blanket, and it was still falling. Icicles hung from the bars across the Victorian lampposts and several inches of snow rested on top of them, like hats.

Grinning, I pulled on my boots then ran downstairs and pulled on my outer-wear.

'This is for you, Liam,' I said, heading into the street and lying down in the middle of the snow, fanning my arms and legs. Holding my phone at arm's length, I took a selfie of my snow angel and sent it to Liam with a message: *Do you remember when we did this in Farmer Duggan's field? Hurry home before the snow melts xx*

I wandered up and down Castle Street taking pictures of other snowy scenes and sending them to him. He probably wouldn't see them until he landed back in the UK, but I wanted Liam to know I was thinking about him. I was *always* thinking about him.

\* \* \*

Tara had been her usual supportive self and had adjusted the rota for The Chocolate Pot so that I could have Lana full-time today through to Thursday and then again on Saturday. I owed her more than a few drinks in the New Year to say thank you. I was confident that Lana would be able to quickly master the basics, freeing me up to work on the complicated activities. That would make such a difference.

'You look tired,' I said when Bethany arrived for work shortly before Lana. Her skin was pale, her eyes were red, and there were dark circles under them.

'I've barely slept for the past week thanks to all the pre-wedding drama. I'm going to need some super amazing concealer for Friday or I'll look more like the bride of Frankenstein than the glowing bride I'm meant to be.'

'Are you sure you don't want to go home and get some rest before the wedding?' I really needed all hands on deck, but I didn't want my sister to make herself ill again. Somehow Lana and I would cope.

Bethany shook her head. 'I'd rather keep myself busy otherwise all I'll think about is Paige and what went wrong with our friendship. I know you said not to waste any more energy on her and I'm trying not to, but we were best friends for seventeen years, or at least I thought we were. I've been talking to the others about it and we've realised there've been incidents over the years when Paige has said or done something nasty, caused problems or even tried to create rifts between us. Who does that and why?'

'I don't know,' I said. 'But remember it was Paige's issue, not yours.'

'That's what Joshua said, but it doesn't stop it hurting.' Bethany shrugged her coat off. 'She's taken far too much of my time recently and you're right that she doesn't deserve it. Anything in particular you need doing this morning?'

'Yes. Cupcakes. In the week leading up to Christmas Day last year, I had a run on them and went through loads of boxes of twelve. A lot of customers take them into work.'

'So we could run out?' Bethany asked, glancing towards the large selection in the shop display cabinet.

'It's possible. I've made more but they need decorating. Do you want...?'

Bethany shook her head vigorously, eyes wide, before I even finished the sentence.

'Okay, message received and understood. I'll see if Lana's any good at it.' I'd previously told Bethany that I'd borrowed Lana as an extra pair of hands, not wanting her to think I'd replaced her immediately.

'The only thing I'm good at in here is making tea so that's what I'll do now.' Bethany headed into the kitchen and filled the kettle.

'I wish you'd stop saying that,' I said. 'There are so many things that you're good at. More than you realise. I still think there's a place for you here so I'm not accepting your resignation. I want to talk to you about an idea I've had, but I've got to finish this cake first.'

'Don't go inventing a role for me,' Bethany said, her expression deadly serious and a hard edge to her voice. 'I won't have it. You've got me for three more days then you're free.' She turned away, indicating that the conversation was over, which was fine because I absolutely had to get on with some work. Plus, it gave me more thinking time.

Finding that card Bethany had made for me years ago had planted a seed of an idea which had gradually grown into something new and exciting. If I could draw all her strengths together into one role, there was definitely a future for my sister at Carly's Cupcakes. Yes, it would be a role I'd invented but it was a role that was needed and one in which she could excel and, in turn, help the business excel. With her current 'I'm a failure' mindset, would she be willing to see it that way? It might take something pretty special to convince her so I needed to fine-tune my proposal before presenting it to her.

* * *

As predicted, the shop side was busy all morning with customers dropping in for cupcakes, usually in large quantities. The snow had stopped falling and the roads had been cleared so it was business as usual for most people.

After a few wobbly attempts, Lana mastered the art of the basic butter icing swirl so keeping the cupcakes stocked became her responsibility. She also seemed adept at the fiddlier work so, between us, we had a production line going to add simple 2D penguins, snowmen and Santa faces to iced cupcakes. If she didn't already work at The Chocolate Pot, I'd have offered her a job on the spot but it wasn't an option. The incident between Paige and Bethany had emphasised the importance of never taking friendships for granted and I wouldn't do anything to jeopardise mine with Tara by poaching her staff. She'd already gone out of her way to help me.

After both Bethany and Lana had taken a lunch break, I announced that I was going to nip out. Bethany looked at me, eyes wide with shock.

'Yes, I know I never take a lunch break but I need to go somewhere. I'll only be about ten minutes, twenty at tops. I'm not expecting any collections until later but I've got my phone with me so ring me if you need me for anything.'

Wrapped up warm, I trudged through the snow to Bear With Me.

'Carly!' Jemma smiled. 'Did you come back to listen to the bears?'

'Something like that,' I said. 'It struck me last night that I made a fleeting visit here when I first opened and I haven't been in since so I fancied a quick break. Am I okay to look round?'

'Of course! Feel free to touch any of the bears but the little ones over there are deceptively heavy so you need to pick them up by their bodies rather than their heads otherwise they cry.' She pointed to a glass display cabinet full of small bears in assorted colours. 'I'll let you browse in peace but shout if you have any questions.'

An older woman appeared from a doorway towards the back of the shop with an armful of teddies and smiled at me before setting about displaying them in a selection of wicker baskets.

It felt magical inside Bear With Me. I wondered whether it was because it was Christmas or whether it felt magical all year round being surrounded by teddy bears. Jemma had certainly created the perfect Christmas atmosphere. Warm white fairy lights hung across the tops of all the shelving units and down the sides of them. Teddy bears hung from or nestled between the branches of a tall tree in one corner and there was a large display of Christmas teddies wearing Santa outfits, elf outfits, or dressed as snowmen.

There was something to see everywhere I looked. I wandered over to the glass cabinet where the smaller bears were and lifted one up.

'Wow! What have you got in here?' I asked, stunned at the weight, despite the warning.

'Steel shot,' Jemma said. 'It weights their bottoms so they sit nicely in position.'

'Jemma makes all of those herself,' said the woman restocking the teddies.

'You really make these yourself, Jemma?' I asked, taking in the intricacies of the different designs.

'The miniature ones you're looking at are all Ju-Sea Jem Bears and they're my designs and the larger ones with the Ju-Sea Bears labels on are the ones my mum makes.'

'Do you make all the little clothes too?'

'Yes. My mum taught me to sew, knit and crochet.'

'Wow! Talented family.'

'Thank you, but you've got your fair share of talent too. I've seen some of your cakes and I've eaten quite a few as well. Seriously impressive stuff.'

I smiled. 'Thank you.' I returned the bear to his spot and focused on the next shelf down. 'Oh my goodness, you've got a bride and groom. My sister's getting married on Friday and she loves bears. These would look amazing on the top of her wedding cake.' I reached into the cabinet and carefully lifted out the pair of jointed bears. 'I don't suppose…? No, it's too last minute. Sorry.'

Jemma joined me. 'Spit it out.'

'It's just that Joshua is Scottish so he's getting married in a kilt. Therefore the bear would ideally wear a kilt but I couldn't ask you to change it for Friday.'

Jemma reached into the back of the cabinet and lifted out a little bear dressed in a Scottish outfit. His kilt was even blue like Joshua's. 'I think our blushing bride has always had her eye on Hamish here so I'm sure there won't be any objections to a little groom-swapping.'

'That would be perfect if you don't mind.'

'It's no problem at all. I can soon make the original groom a new bride. I'll take these over to the till but feel free to finish looking round and ask the bears your question.'

I moved onto the next display cabinet containing the larger bears made by Jemma's mum. 'Oh my goodness, he's gorgeous.' I lifted out a cream bear tangled up in fairy lights with the cutest expression on his face, as though resigned to the fact that things like that always happened to him.

'That's Tangled,' Jemma said, 'for obvious reasons. Mum only finished him yesterday.'

'Aw, he's just like my sister. She manages to get tangled in the Christmas lights every year. I made a penguin-shaped Christmas cake for a customer recently and he was tangled in lights like this – the penguin, that is, not the customer – and it made me think of Bethany.' I thought of the proposal I wanted to make to Bethany. Could Tangled help me convince her? If not, he'd be a more meaningful personal Christmas gift than anything I'd bought her already.

'I'll take him too,' I said, 'and now I'd better step away from the bears before they all end up coming home with me.'

I handed over my debit card after Jemma rang the purchases through the till. As I waited for the payment to process, I studied the wall behind her. Beautifully hand-illustrated teddy bear pictures were hung in frames with accompanying bear-related phrases such as, 'You're never too old for a bear,' and 'A bear hug a day keeps the dark skies away.'

'A friend of mine makes them,' Jemma said, following my gaze. 'He normally draws for comic books but he's very talented at drawing bears too.'

'They're lovely.' My eyes narrowed as the words 'heart's desire' jumped out at me on another of the pictures. '"Achieving your heart's desire starts with a big hug",' I read. Instantly I pictured myself hugging Liam and how the hugs always seemed to linger. We'd properly hold each other and not just when he'd been away for months and I was welcoming him home. I'd always held onto him longer because I loved him and hadn't wanted to let him go, but why had he held onto me for longer than normal? Could it mean that he felt the same way about me and always had done?

'It's actually a bit of a play on words,' Jemma said, refocussing my attention. 'A collection of bears is called a hug.'

'Is it? That's so cute.'

Jemma nodded. 'Isn't it? And now you've started your sister's collectible hug for her. A new hug, a new husband, and a lovely sister. She's a lucky girl.'

'She isn't feeling very lucky at the minute. That dark skies phrase is perfect for her.'

'We've got it in a card,' Jemma said.

'Really? Can I have one?'

'On the house,' she said, popping one into the bag with the bears. 'I hope it does the trick in cheering your sister up.'

'So do I,' I said. 'Thank you so much, Jemma.'

'What are you two giggling at?' I asked when I returned to the shop. I'd left my purchases with Jemma who'd kindly offered to drop them off after Bethany had finished for the day.

'Lana was telling me about what that creep Jasper did,' Bethany said. 'I can't believe the nerve of the guy.'

'Bethany came up with a great suggestion to drop him in it.' Lana handed me her phone. 'I put this on Instagram.'

Bethany had taken a photo of Lana behind the till, looking like she was serving some cupcakes. Beside that image were two smaller photos – one of some of the Christmas cupcakes that Lana had decorated that morning and one of the cake I'd made for Jasper's daughter's christening. On the post, she'd typed: *Having an awesome time working in @CarlysCupcakes. Carly let me have a go at icing some today and they're not too shabby. She's super talented. Look at the cake she made for my baby cousin's christening. She stayed up really late doing this last minute because my Uncle Jasper had completely forgotten to order one, the numpty!*

Laughing, I handed the phone back to Lana. 'That's naughty, but thank you. I love it.'

'She tagged Jasper in,' Bethany said.

'And Auntie Andrea,' Lana added. 'She's already commented on it asking if it's true. Uncle Jasper is in so much trouble and it serves him right.'

'Thank you again,' I said. 'I hope he learns a lesson from it.' Feeling avenged by their mischief-making, I grinned to myself as I headed towards the workshop.

'Oh! A girl came in to see you,' Bethany called. 'She said she'd come back later.'

I stopped in the archway. 'Did she leave her name?'

'No. We checked if she was collecting an order, but she said she wasn't.'

I shrugged. 'Probably someone wanting to see if I have any jobs going. When she comes back, can you ask her if that's what she wants and tell her that I don't have any vacancies?'

'But you do,' Bethany said.

I shook my head. 'I'm still determined to make you stay.'

'Not gonna happen and, as I said before, I'm not having you invent a role you don't need.'

'We'll see.'

I set to work on my afternoon's task of a really simple but last minute Christmas cake order – a plain white cake with a purple ribbon round it. I'd made and iced the cake but I needed to make purple, silver and white snowflakes to scatter across it. I was cutting out the fiddly snowflakes when Bethany appeared in the archway.

'That girl's back and she says she isn't looking for a job and she does need to speak to you. She says she knows you're busy and promises that it won't take long.'

'Okay, I'll come through.' I wiped my hands down my apron and wandered into the shop. A girl who looked a little younger than Lana was bent down looking at the cupcake designs in the cabinet.

'Hi, I'm Carly. You wanted to see me?'

She straightened up. 'Hi, yes. I wanted to say thank you for my cake.'

I smiled. 'You're very welcome but would that be any cake in particular?'

The girl giggled nervously. 'Sorry. I'm being stupid. My name's Trinity and my mum got you to make a cake for me...'

Trinity? Trinity? My mind whirred. Where had I heard that name recently?

'...based on a drawing of a penguin that I'd done for my art exam.'

Eek! That was it. Joanna Osborne's daughter. The angry customer. I glanced nervously across at Bethany.

'The penguin with the fairy lights tangled in his reindeer antlers?' Bethany asked. 'I loved that cake. You designed that?'

Trinity beamed proudly. 'Yes. His name's Percy.' She reached into her bag and took out a picture in a wooden frame. 'I wanted to give you this. I can't give you the original because it's for my course-work but I copied him and I took a photo of the cake.' She handed me the frame. Written on the cartoon was: *An original design by Trinity Osborne lovingly brought to life by Carly's Cupcakes.*

'That's so lovely,' I said, feeling genuinely touched. 'Thank you. I'll put this up in the shop if that's okay with you.'

'I'd love that,' Trinity said. 'It's also an apology gift.'

My heart sank. Oh no! Trinity was about to spill the beans. 'There's no need,' I said. 'It was a misunderstanding and it's all sorted now. Thanks for this. Have a great Christmas.'

But Bethany wasn't going to let Trinity go without an explanation. 'An apology for what?' she asked.

'The picture got posted on social media by mistake and I saw it before the cake was collected,' Trinity said. She turned to me. 'I'm sorry my mum had a go at you.'

'It was nothing.'

'I doubt it. She was hopping mad when she left home. She's got such a short fuse. I know she'll have shouted at you, which wasn't fair.'

I shrugged, trying to make light of it, but the damage was done. Although I was trying not to look at Bethany, I could see her shocked expression out of my peripheral vision. 'You'd had a tough time recently. She was trying to protect you.'

'A tough time? I have not!' Trinity shook her head, frowning. 'Oh, there was a minor issue at school at the end of last term but it all got sorted. My mum can be such a drama queen when she wants to be.'

'Your mum said some friends accused you of copying the penguin and you were in tears...?' I said, realising too late that I was making things worse from Bethany's perspective.

Trinity rolled her eyes. 'My bestie put a comment on Instagram joking about inspiration coming from all sorts of places and a winky face. She knew I'd designed it from scratch cos she was with me at the time. Sorry. More unnecessary drama on my mum's part. And I'm sorry about those awful rants she put online. At least they're gone now.'

When Trinity finally left, I turned to face a straight-faced Bethany, cringing.

'Why didn't you tell me?' she demanded.

'It wasn't your fault. I hadn't told you that I don't put photos online until the customer has collected the order and confirmed that I'm okay to do so.'

Bethany shook her head. 'It doesn't matter. It was still my fault because all you'd asked me to do was take some photos and I didn't follow your instructions.'

'It was fine.'

'Of course it wasn't fine,' Bethany cried. 'A customer comes in and yells at you. How is that fine?'

'I handled it. I explained that it was a mistake and she went away happy in the end.'

'Happy?' Bethany gasped. 'Oh no! How much discount did you have to give her?'

My cheeks reddened and I lowered my eyes.

'No! You gave it away for free, didn't you? You put hours and hours into that cake and you gave it away for free because of me.' She barged past me towards the workshop.

'Where are you going?' I glanced at Lana who grimaced and looked like she wished the ground would swallow her up.

Moments later, Bethany reappeared with her coat and bag. 'What did she put online?' she demanded.

'I don't know. I got her to remove the posts in exchange for...' I tailed off. I wasn't helping matters.

Bethany nodded, her jaw tight. 'So I managed to ruin your reputation as well as wasting your time and money?'

'You weren't to know. I should have told you.'

She shook her head again and marched towards the door. 'I need to leave now before I completely destroy your business.'

'No! Don't go! I've got a proposition for you.'

'Stop it, Carly!' she cried, striding back towards the counter. 'Just stop it! You're my sister and I love you but you have got to stop it with this eternal optimism about me. I'm a failure at every single thing I try. I fail at jobs, I fail at friendships and my future in-laws hate me and that's because they can see me for what I really am.' Her voice had raised in pitch and volume and she was trembling.

She turned and stormed towards the door again and stopped with her hand on the handle. 'They're right.' She turned to face me. 'I'm not good enough for Joshua. They know that my marriage will fail because everything I touch does, so I might as well call it off. What was I thinking of, believing that I could do one thing in my life correctly?'

She yanked the door open then slammed it behind her.

I dived for the door and out onto the snow-covered cobbles.

'Bethany!' I called. 'Bethany!' But she was already lost in the crowds of Christmas shoppers. I pressed a shaking hand to my lips. This was bad. Very bad.

## 15

'Do you want me to run after her?' Lana asked when I stepped back into the shop and closed the door. Eyes wide and pale-faced, she looked pretty shaken.

I gave her what I hoped was a reassuring smile. 'No. Thank you, though. She's just a bit stressed and emotional with the wedding being so close. She'll be fine by the morning.' My words sounded convincing, but I didn't believe them. Something about this time felt very different.

'Is there anything I can do?'

'You could pop the kettle on,' I suggested. 'I'm just going to ring her fiancé.'

Lana nodded and scuttled into the workshop.

'I'm sure she'll have just gone home, made herself a cuppa and calmed down,' I said, after I'd updated Joshua.

'Are you trying to convince me or yourself?' he asked, demonstrating the maturity beyond his years that acted as such a good balance to Bethany's bouts of immaturity.

I sighed. 'I don't know what to think, Joshua. She's had strops before but this was like a full-blown meltdown. I think it might have been building up for a while. I should have done more to help her.'

'You've done loads and I know she's really grateful for it. I'm in York just now and there's some stuff I have to do but I can probably get away within the hour. I'll call you when I get home or if I hear from her in the meantime.'

We said our goodbyes and disconnected the call. York was about an hour's drive away which meant up to two hours of Bethany being alone. The idea didn't sit comfortably with me but what could I do? She was an adult and she needed to make her own decisions. Being overly protective towards her for all these years probably hadn't helped with the way she responded to challenging situations.

\* \* \*

It was hard to concentrate on my tasks that afternoon and I had to re-work several pieces after making careless mistakes. When Joshua rang shortly after 4.30 p.m., my stomach churned in nervous anticipation.

'She's gone,' he said the moment I answered, his voice flat.

'What do mean gone?' My heart started racing.

'She left a wee note. It says, "Your parents were right. I'm not good enough for you and you're going to realise this sooner or later. I love you but I mess up everything and I'm bound to mess up our marriage so I'm getting out of your life before I do. I'll send for the rest of my stuff when I'm settled somewhere. Take care".' His voice broke as a sob escaped. 'She's taken some of her clothes and her car's gone.'

A wave of nausea swept through me and I sank back in my chair, gulping in air. 'Oh, Joshua. I'm so sorry,' I finally managed to mumble. 'I never imagined—' But I couldn't finish the sentence. I couldn't find the words. What was her state of mind to have walked out on the man she loved? I shuddered and took a deep breath. 'I should have done more to convince her not to leave the shop.'

He cleared his throat. 'It's not your fault, Carly. Nobody could have known it was going to build up to a full-on meltdown like this. Bollocks! I don't know what to do. She's not answering her phone and I can't think of anywhere she'd go.'

'Have you rung my parents?' I asked.

'Not yet.'

'Do you want me to call them? She could have gone there.'

'Yes, please. But I don't think she'll be there. I think she's properly gone.' His voice cracked again. 'What if she never comes back?'

My heart broke for him. 'She will,' I said gently. 'She loves you. She said so in her note, didn't she? She's just lost her way and needs some time out. We'll find her and we'll get her some help.'

'I love her so much,' he said.

'I know you do. You two were made for each other. She'll come home. Try not to worry.' Once more, my words sounded convincing but I didn't feel convinced. What if she didn't come home? She could be really stubborn when her mind was set on something.

'I'll never forgive my parents if anything happens to her,' he said, his voice full of bitterness.

'It won't. She just needs some space. There'll be a wedding on Friday, I promise you.' I crossed my fingers, desperately hoping this was a promise I could fulfil.

'I just want her back. I don't care if the wedding goes ahead or not as long as I have my Bethany. I can't live without her. She's my life.'

I swallowed hard on the lump in my throat. There couldn't be another man alive more deserving of my sister and I knew the feeling was mutual which was why her walking out was so worrying.

'I think you need to call your parents,' I said, trying to sound strong. 'I know you're angry with them and that's understandable but the fight with your mum was one of many recent incidents so it's not fair to put all the blame on them. You need their support right now. You can have words with them later but, for now, focus on finding Bethany.'

He sighed. 'You're right.'

We ended the call and I phoned Mum, catching her as she was leaving work. She phoned back as soon as she got home to report that Bethany wasn't there and there was no indication that she had been.

'I've called your dad but he hasn't heard from her,' Mum said, her voice edged with worry. 'Neither of us can think where she could have gone. I presume you've tried her friends?'

'I phoned her bridesmaids while you were driving home but none of them have heard from her. They're going to contact some other friends and keep me posted. I even called Paige, not that I'd have expected Bethany to turn to her after what happened.'

Mum sighed. 'I heard about that. To think we've welcomed that girl into our family since she was six years old. I can't believe it.'

'I know. I think it's hit Bethany hard. I'm going to have to crack on, Mum, but I'll keep ringing her and can you and Dad do the same?'

'Of course we will. Try not to worry. I'm sure she'll be back once she's calmed down.'

The bell tinkled in the shop and I realised it was past closing time and I hadn't even locked up. 'There's a customer. I've got to go. Bye, Mum.'

I stepped into the shop with a fake smile on my face but relaxed when I saw it was Jemma from Bear With Me dropping off the bears. Thanking her, I peeked into the bag and the tears started at the sight of Tangled nestled in the bottom on a bed of tissue paper with the bride and groom seated between his legs.

'Oh my God! Are you okay?' Jemma asked.

'Sorry. It's just...' And it all spilled out.

When I'd finished explaining, she hugged me, telling me to let her know if there was anything she could do to help. What could she do, though? Bethany had left of her own freewill. She wasn't a missing person.

Ten minutes later, Tara knocked on the door. 'Jemma stopped by and told me what happened so I'm here to help. What have you done so far?'

'What sort of car does she drive?' she asked when I'd told her who I'd contacted.

'It's an old yellow Ford Ka.'

'Should be easy to spot.' Tara looked at her watch. 'Give me fifteen minutes to clear up at the café then I'll drive round town and check all the car parks. If I wanted to clear my head, I'd probably drive along the seafront and maybe park up somewhere on The Headland so I'll try there first.'

'Should I come with you?'

She shook her head. 'No, you need to stay here in case she calls or comes back. I'm assuming Joshua's stayed at home?'

'Yes. His parents have driven round the streets near the house but I think the car parks are a better idea. Thank you.'

* * *

A few hours later, Tara returned to Carly's Cupcakes, her expression grim. She'd explored pretty much every inch of Whitsborough Bay and had nothing to report. No yellow cars. No Bethany.

'Do you want me to stay with you?' she asked.

I shook my head. 'I appreciate the offer, though. Mum and Dad are out looking and they're going to call in with a takeaway, not that I feel like eating.'

'I know it's easier said than done but try not to worry. Sometimes bad things happen and people just need to be alone while they get their head in order. She'll get in touch when she's ready.'

She hugged me then said goodbye and I wondered whether she was speaking from experience. Had something bad happened to her to make her leave London?

Mum and Dad arrived shortly afterwards. They both looked exhausted. Mum had driven round town and then south down the coast to Fellingthorpe. Dad had driven up the coast to Whitby – somewhere we'd loved to visit as a family when we were younger – but to no avail.

'It was a long shot,' he said, rubbing his eyes, 'but we had to try something.'

We took the Chinese takeaway up to the flat and, even though Dad declared that we all needed to eat, he didn't manage more than a few mouthfuls before dropping his fork and pushing his plate away.

'I think we'd better get home in case she shows up there,' Mum said.

I tried to sound upbeat when they hugged me goodbye and told me I should get some sleep. It was obvious they were worried about Bethany and that was without knowing everything that had happened. Bethany had told them about the incident with Paige but some subtle probing made it apparent that they had no idea about her storming out last week, being ill, or the bust-up with Joshua's parents. Therefore only Joshua and I knew how fragile she'd been over the last week or so and now wasn't the time to share that.

\* \* \*

My phone rang at 2.40 a.m. Unable to contemplate sleep, I was curled up on the sofa in front of the fire, wrapped in a fluffy throw. 'Bethany?' I grabbed my phone, but it was Liam's name on the screen. Despite everything, my heart leapt.

'I picked up your messages,' he said, his voice full of concern. 'Any news?'

'No and I'm frantic with worry. Are you home?'

'Not quite. I made a detour. Come to the window.'

I dashed to the window and peeked through the wooden blinds, butterflies swirling in my stomach as Liam stepped away from the shop doorway and into the lamplight. He raised his hand in greeting and I clapped my hand across my mouth, muffling a sound which was somewhere between a squeal and a sob.

'I'm coming down,' I cried.

A multitude of emotions swirled through me as I ran down the stairs and through the shop. Liam was back! The man I'd secretly loved for the whole of my adult life was actually here and I was going to be able to hold him and speak to him for longer than a few snatched minutes.

'Am I glad to see you.' I flung myself at him the second I opened the door.

He dropped his backpack and held me tightly, whispering reassurances. I felt so safe in his arms, like I'd always done, and I believed him when he said that Bethany would be safe and everything would be fine. With Liam back, it felt like everything really could be.

It was with great reluctance that I pulled away. 'We'd better get you inside and warmed up,' I said, ushering him in before closing and locking the door. 'The fire's on upstairs.'

Liam left his backpack in the shop and followed me up the internal stairs and into the lounge. 'I've always loved this room,' he said, kicking off his boots. 'It's so cosy.'

It was a large room with a high ceiling, but a warm colour

palette, fairy lights all year round, candles, and a real fire kept it cosy. My Christmas tree stood in the bay window, covered in more twinkling lights and surrounded by wrapped gifts. I always had my gifts purchased and wrapped by early November, knowing the shop would get too busy to even think about Christmas shopping once December hit.

Liam curled up on the opposite end of the two-seater sofa to me while, over a mug of tea, I filled him in on the events of the past week or so. I could feel the heat from his body where his leg rested against mine, sending tingles of excitement up and down me.

'It sounds like you've done everything you can so far,' he said, placing his mug on the floor beside the sofa and trying to stifle a yawn. 'The best thing you can do right now is get some sleep and it's time I left you alone so you can do that.'

He stood up and stretched. His eyes were bloodshot and he had to be shattered. The flight from Kabul to London was nearly eight hours so, with the travel either side, he'd probably been on the move for double that.

'Thanks so much for coming straight here,' I said, standing up and reaching for his hand, my heart racing as his fingers entwined with mine.

'Where else would I go?' He spoke so tenderly and looked at me with such concern, tears rushed to my eyes.

'I really do appreciate it. You're exactly what I need.' I held my breath, wondering how he'd take the comment.

'I'll always be here for you.' He smiled and those cornflower-blue eyes that had always mesmerised me twinkled, despite the obvious fatigue. There were white laughter crinkles round them on an otherwise deeply tanned complexion and the dessert sun had bleached the front of his hair so light that it was almost white. I swear he grew more handsome every time I saw him but my attraction had never been about his looks. I'd fallen in love with his big, kind heart. I'd fallen in love with the geeky, lanky kid who got teased at school. I'd fallen in love with my best friend.

An overwhelming need not to say goodbye swept through me. It wasn't the time for a big confession but I longed to have him near me. I bit my lip. 'Will you stay with me tonight?'

There was a pause and I could hear my own heart thumping rapidly.

'You want me to?' It was said with hesitation rather than surprise. Was he testing the water, waiting to see if I took it further?

I nodded and we stood in silence for a moment, staring at each other, drinking each other in. His hand was still in mine. All it would take was one step forward and a massive dose of courage and I could kiss him. Could I? Should I?

A log moving in the fire made a loud crackle and broke the moment.

'Have you got a spare duvet?' Liam asked, letting go of my hand.

I shook my head while my heart raced even faster. 'No, but I've got a king size bed and I could do with a hug.'

* * *

I'd never felt nervous in Liam's presence but, as I brushed my teeth and pulled on my PJs, I couldn't stop trembling. We'd never shared a bed before. We'd shared a small tent – a much more confined space than my bed – on numerous occasions but the prospect of cuddling up under the duvet without the fabric of a sleeping bag separating us was both thrilling and terrifying.

I needn't have worried. I emerged from the bathroom to find Liam lying on his side in a mock-seductive Austin Powers style pose. He gave a growl, cried 'yeah, baby', then patted the space beside him. I'd missed the laughter so much.

'The hug's ready when you are,' he said as I slipped under the duvet.

I gratefully snuggled against his broad chest and he wrapped his arms round me. 'She'll be fine,' he said, kissing the top of my head. 'She's a fighter and always has been but sometimes even the greatest fighters get defeated. And you know what happens next? They pick themselves up and get back in the ring and that's what Bethany will do too.'

'What would I do without you?' I asked, squeezing him.

'You'll never be without me. Me and you against the world, remember? Always.'

I lay against him for several minutes, listening to the steady thump of his heartbeat.

'Will you take my mind off Bethany?' I asked eventually. 'Tell me about your friends in Afghanistan.'

'They're good lads but not a patch on my best friend.'

'Yes, well, that would be impossible. She is, after all, the most fantastic person in the whole of the world.'

He laughed as he twiddled with a strand of my hair. 'She certainly is. So, let's tell you about the troops.'

I could have listened to him talking all night, his gentle voice soothing me. If only every night could be like that.

## 16

I didn't expect to sleep a wink but I'd certainly been in a deep sleep when my mobile started to ring shortly before 7.00 a.m. Whether it was the comfort of having Liam curled up beside me or whether I was downright exhausted, I wasn't sure.

'Bethany?' I muttered, eyes too blurry to focus on the screen.

'It's Joshua. Have you slept?'

I rubbed my eyes. 'Not much. You?'

Liam was sound asleep and I didn't want to disturb him so I slipped out of bed, pulled on my dressing gown and padded through to the lounge.

'A couple of hours, I think,' Joshua said. 'I wish she'd call. I don't mind if she's not ready to come home yet, but I need to know she's all right.'

'I know. Me too.' I parted the blinds and looked out over Castle Street. 'It's snowing again.'

'It started a couple of hours ago,' he said. 'You don't think she could be broken down somewhere in this, do you?'

'No. Bethany may be emotional but she's not daft. She'll have checked into a B&B.'

'I hope so.' Joshua sighed. 'Sorry for waking you up so early.'

'It's fine. I'm usually up and working before now anyway.' My stomach clenched at the thought of how far behind I now was and whether, for the first time ever, I was going to have to let customers down.

After I said goodbye to Joshua, I tiptoed back towards my bedroom. Liam was sprawled out on his stomach, completely out of it. He probably hadn't slept for the preceding twenty-four hours; possibly longer. I watched him breathing, feeling comforted by the rise and fall of the duvet, but work called. Tearing my gaze away from him, I went to the bathroom to wash and dress. Ideally I'd have showered and washed my hair but time was not on my side and a quick spruce with a can of dry shampoo would have to suffice. I scribbled a note for Liam and left it on my side of the bed: *Downstairs but don't rush if you need more sleep x*

I made my way down to the workshop and texted Lana to ask if there was any chance she could come in earlier and help with the cupcakes. Ninety minutes extra from her would massively help.

Putting the kettle on for what I suspected would be the first of several strong coffees, I dug out my weekly planner. My hands shook as I studied it, swiftly calculating exactly how far behind I was. It was an absolute disaster. I'd be able to make what I needed for collections today but it was the rest of the week that was going to cause a huge problem. I wasn't sure what Liam had planned but I was going to need his help and even that, plus the extra hours from Lana, was unlikely to be enough to get back on track. My reputation, which I'd spent over four years building up, was on the brink. That thought, accompanied by worry about Bethany, made me want to curl up into a ball and sob, but I knew I had to remain strong and focused. I took a deep breath, washed my hands, switched the oven on and gathered the ingredients to make the first batch of cupcakes.

* * *

Lana was making great progress with decorating the daily cupcakes and I was rolling out the icing for a Christmas cake being collected that afternoon when Liam's footsteps on the stairs made my heart thump. The bell tinkled as he reached the bottom so Lana disappeared into the shop to see to the customer.

'Oh my God, Carls, your bed is so comfortable.' Liam wrapped his arms round me from behind and pressed his cheek against mine. It was a friendly gesture he'd done many times before but it suddenly felt so intimate. My breath caught and I felt quite light-headed for a moment as his stubble lightly grazed my cheek and I breathed in the fresh smell of toothpaste, ocean-scented body spray and soap.

When he added, 'I could stay here forever,' I gulped and had to fight back the urge to respond with, 'Then why don't you?'

He straightened up and I took a deep breath, trying to compose myself.

'Any word on Bethany?' he asked.

'Nothing new. I spoke to Joshua first thing and he's doing his best to hold it together but he's a wreck.'

'And you?'

'Doing my best to hold it together, also a wreck, and bricking it because I'm too far behind to recover. At some point, I'm going to have to decide which customers I have to let down.' A wave of panic made me shudder.

'What can I do to help?' he asked, placing his strong hands on my shoulders, instantly calming me.

I pressed my cheek against one of his hands. 'I can't ask you to help. You haven't even been home yet.'

He removed his hands and crouched down beside me. 'You

don't need to ask. It's already a done deal. I've spoken to Mum and she sends her love.'

I adored Liam's parents. Like mine, they'd always been supportive of our friendship.

'If you're sure about staying, you could make another batch of cupcakes for me.' Lana was going to do some but the shop had been too busy. I'd created some space so she could ice the cooled-down cupcakes between serving so at least she'd been able to do some multi-tasking.

'I haven't made cupcakes since food tech at school. I seem to remember not being too shabby at it.'

I smiled at him, remembering. 'You were actually better than me which is kind of embarrassing given my career choice. So that's your job today but let me introduce you to Lana first.'

Somehow, we made it through the afternoon but I couldn't have done it without Lana and Liam. Lana worked her socks off. She decorated and restocked cupcakes, and helped out with some of the simple decorations for my cakes while Liam became chief baker and washer-upper.

All the Tuesday collections were ready on time, even though one was a close shave with me securing an iced figure in place only thirty seconds before the customer walked through the door.

Despite his protests, I insisted that Liam went home for a couple of hours during the afternoon to at least say hello to his parents. He relented but was back just over an hour later in a fresh set of clothes, telling me that he had plenty of time to catch up with them properly later and that his mum had offered use of her oven if things got tight at the shop, which was a lovely gesture.

'As long as you need me, I'll be here for you,' Liam said, his gaze steadfast.

My stomach did another backflip at the intensity of his look and I wondered if there was more to the words. It felt like something had shifted between us both since he'd come home but that could have been down to my heightened emotional state and a lot of wishful thinking on my part.

'I need you,' I whispered.

'Then I'm all yours.' He kept holding my gaze and I had that sensation once more that it would only take a small movement from one of us and we'd be kissing, but my phone ringing distracted us and we lost the moment again.

My phone never seemed to stop ringing. I took calls from my parents, Joshua, Bethany's friends, and more cake enquiries using the promotion code that I couldn't quite place but hadn't had time to check. Sadly, there was no word from the one person from whom I really wanted to hear.

* * *

'How's the planner looking?' Liam asked, sitting down beside me at the workshop table as I ticked off another task shortly after 4.30 p.m.

I exhaled loudly as I slowly shook my head.

'That bad, eh?'

'Worse.' I rolled my stiff shoulders.

'Aching?' he asked.

'Every inch of me aches.'

Liam stood up, moved behind me and began to gently massage my shoulders, sending a tingle of delight up and down my spine.

'You have no idea how good that is,' I whispered. I could feel my eyes closing as my body relaxed. 'It's so good that I'm going to have to ask you to stop or I'll fall asleep and face plant this cake.'

'What else can I do to help?' he asked, sitting down beside me again.

'You've done so much already. Are you sure you don't want to go home?'

'The only place I want to be is here with you,' he said. That intense look was there once more. Butterflies flitted in my stomach. *Be brave. Tell him that's where you want him to be.*

'Carly! Customer for you,' called Lana.

Liam picked up the planner as I apologised and headed into the shop, cursing yet another lost moment.

I shooed Lana out of the door at five when the shop closed. She offered to stay longer but I wasn't having it. 'You've worked an extra-long day as it is and I can't tell you how much I appreciate that. If you can come in early again tomorrow, though, I'd be ever so grateful.'

She nodded enthusiastically. 'I can be here for half eight. I've really enjoyed today. I loved making those little penguins.'

'You have a natural talent for it,' I said. I suspected that Lana could have done a lot more but I couldn't spare the time to show her how to make anything other than the simplest figures.

As I locked the door, a thought struck me and my stomach sank. I dashed back through to the workshop to where Liam was wiping the table. 'We were supposed to be going out for a meal tonight and I can't... I just can't. I'm so sorry. I have to get these orders ready or...' Having held it together all day, my voice had risen towards hysteria and I could feel myself on the verge of losing it.

Liam rushed to my side and held me close. 'Hey, don't let those tears fall. It'll all work out. I thought we could order a takeaway pizza tonight and go out another night when things are calmer. Eating in or eating out doesn't matter to me, as long as the company's good.'

I squeezed him gratefully, the tears retreating. 'You always know the right things to say.'

A knock on the door made us break apart.

'Ooh, wonder who that could be?' Liam said, sounding all mysterious.

'What's going on?' I asked, eyeing him suspiciously.

He gave an exaggerated shrug. 'I have *no* idea but I think you'd better get the door.'

I wandered back through to the shop, unlocked the door and jumped at the cry of, 'Surprise!'

'What are you all doing here?' I asked, looking from one smiling face to the next.

'We heard there might be a cake icing pizza party going on and it sounded like the perfect way to spend a Tuesday night,' Tara said.

'Let us in,' Sarah called. 'It's freezing out here.'

I ushered the collection of Castle Street business owners inside – Tara, Ginny from The Wedding Emporium, Sarah from Seaside Blooms and Jemma from Bear With Me.

'Annie from my team is on standby,' Jemma said. 'She can be here for seven if we need her.'

'And Cathy can be here in an hour if we need her too,' Sarah said, referring to one of her team, 'although we thought you might be struggling for space if there were too many of us.'

The dam burst and tears flowed at the kindness of the group, especially Jemma whom I didn't even know that well. I turned to face Liam, wiping my cheeks. 'You organised this?'

'It was Tara,' he said. 'I ran the idea past her and she rounded up the troops. I know it may take some organising but surely there are things we can all do to help.'

'Oh my goodness, there certainly are. Thank you all so very, very much.'

'Would some more tables help?' Tara asked. 'I can get some from the café and set them up in here.'

'That would be perfect,' I said. 'There's definitely not enough space for us all in the workshop and kitchen.'

'Right, gang, dump your bags and let's go next door to get some tables and leave our new boss to work out what she needs us to do.' Tara opened the door again and they filed out.

'Do you need another hand?' Liam called after them.

'No. You look after Carly,' Tara said. 'I think she might need a hug.' The door closed.

'Do you?' Liam asked, stepping closer to me, that intense look in his eyes once more.

'Always,' I whispered, blinking back the fresh supply of tears.

As I relaxed into his hold, I thought about the sign in Jemma's shop: *Achieving your heart's desire starts with a big hug.* My heart's desire was holding me right now and there was no place I'd rather be. All it would take was for me to raise my head slightly and I'd be in the perfect position to kiss Liam. Would he respond or would he push me off, an expression of shock on his face that I'd dared to breach our friendship? What was he thinking? Was he wondering about kissing me too or about how shattered he was and how he really didn't want to be spending the evening cutting out icing snowflakes and rolling snowmen's bodies? My stomach sank. Why was I even thinking about Liam and me when the only reason we were stuck in the shop for the evening instead of going out for a meal was because I was behind with my work? And the reason I was behind with my work was that Bethany was missing and nobody knew where she was. It was hardly great timing for exploring a relationship with Liam. It was time to let him go and focus on organising the evening's work. I couldn't do anything to bring Bethany back but I did have the power to avoid any further damage to the reputation of Carly's Cupcakes. Telling Liam how I felt could wait. It had waited years already so a few more days wouldn't make any difference.

My phone rang, naturally breaking the hug. Hope flickered through me then my heart sank again when it was Tara's name instead of Bethany's that flashed on the screen.

'Hello?'

'Do you want some mixing bowls or anything like that?' she asked.

'Yes, please. Bowls, rolling pins, spoons, sharp knives. Whatever might be useful. Thanks.'

I disconnected the call and looked up at Liam. 'They'll be back soon.'

'I'd better let you get organised, then.' He gave me a half smile. Did he look disappointed? I wasn't sure.

## 17

It was no mean feat organising five cake-decorating novices but I somehow managed to get a system going. Liam had already proved himself great at baking cakes so that remained his domain. Tara and Sarah based themselves in the shop side and assumed responsibility for rolling out icing and cutting out shapes using templates or cutters. Jemma offered to help me with the more complicated pieces and, with space at a premium, Ginny did a supermarket run, armed with a shopping list of baking ingredients.

At first, there were frequent peals of laughter as mistakes were made. Outwardly, I grinned good naturedly as Tara scraped icing off the table, Sarah dropped several items on the floor and Jemma created some very deformed characters. Inwardly, panic steadily rose. Was this going to be one of those occasions where too many cooks spoiled the broth? Thankfully, the creativity they all demonstrated in their businesses kicked in, they settled into their roles and the team became incredibly productive. Tara and Sarah both showed an aptitude for rolling out the icing to the correct thickness and Jemma's skills at working with miniature teddy bears translated into making icing figurines so I could let her get on with the simpler ones and focus on the more complicated tasks myself.

Ginny returned with the shopping and paused on the shop side. 'How long have I been gone?' she exclaimed. 'You've done loads.'

She made her way through to the workshop and placed the bags on the floor before checking on progress at our table. 'Did you make those, Jem?'

Jemma nodded. 'Took me a few attempts but Carly's a brilliant tutor.'

'They're amazing.' She squeezed my shoulder. 'Novices to professionals in less than an hour. Definitely a brilliant tutor.'

They were exactly the words I needed to hear and I smiled at her gratefully. 'They're the brilliant ones, giving up their time like this.'

My smile widened at the cries of being happy to help, having fun, and always being there for a friend in need. I swallowed on the lump constricting my throat. All my life, it had just been Liam and me against the world, used to being the outsiders who nobody except our families cared about. Right now, these four women were also my world and I would be forever grateful to them for being there to help save my business.

Ginny put the shopping away, put some Christmas music on, then flitted between washing up, getting items from the storeroom, and helping wherever she was needed.

Shortly after 8.00 p.m., pizzas arrived and we all took a well-earned break. Having barely eaten the night before, I was ravenous and evidently the others were too as the first couple of slices each were eaten in relative silence with only appreciative noises at how delicious the food was.

Tara turned to Liam and asked, 'What was Carly like when she was younger?'

He smiled at me warmly, his twinkling eyes making my insides all gooey.

'Carls was and always will be the best thing that ever happened to me.' Then he winked and turned to the group. 'And I have to thank her for a back catalogue of hilarious mishaps that have kept me going on the darkest of days overseas.'

'Which you're now going to share with us, of course,' Sarah prompted, grinning.

'Of course!'

I cringed. 'No, Liam! You're not going to tell them—'

'About the time you left the tent open and a goat ate your knickers?' he suggested, eyes sparkling with mischief.

The anecdotes kept coming and my sides soon ached from laughing – something I'd never have predicted could happen earlier in the day. Liam never needed to embellish the truth because he had a gift for story-telling. Accents, facial expressions and dramatic pauses captivated his new audience and transported me right back to the occasion itself. I'd even forgotten about some of the tales he told.

'I can't believe you can remember all those stories in such detail,' I said, nudging him playfully.

He fixed his eyes on mine and his expression was so tender, my heart raced again. 'I remember everything about being with you.'

The tension between us crackled and he must have suddenly registered we weren't alone because he turned away with a nervous chuckle and addressed the group. 'Did she tell you about the time she got the hiccups in the middle of school assembly?'

They all laughed as he relayed the story but Tara caught my eye. She gave a slight incline of her head towards Liam, then me, then discreetly raised her thumb. There was no doubt in her meaning – she thought he had feelings for me too – and my insides went all gooey again.

It was astonishing how calm and relaxed I felt as I cleared away the pizza boxes, especially considering the workload I had. The break and especially the laughter had been much-needed and both were way overdue, but work needed to resume.

'I hate to break up the party...' I said.

'Such a hard task-master,' Tara joked. 'She runs an even tighter ship than me.'

* * *

Ninety minutes later, I downed tools and stretched my arms above my head. 'It's past ten and I'm sure you're all ready for your beds. I think we've finally caught up.'

Ginny looked up from her latest task of decorating cupcakes. 'Catching up is amazing but I'm happy to do another hour or so if that will get you ahead.'

'You've done so much already,' I protested.

'I'm good to stay,' Tara called from the shop.

'Me too,' Sarah added.

'I'm a night owl anyway,' Jemma said. 'What's next?'

I didn't protest because the thought of getting ahead filled me with such relief. There was still no word from Bethany and, unless she got in touch later tonight or first thing, I'd likely lose some time tomorrow worrying about her and phoning round her friends once more.

Sarah and Ginny stayed for another hour and Tara and Jemma pulled their coats on ready to leave shortly before midnight.

'I can't thank you enough,' I said as I hugged Jemma goodbye. 'I'd have had to cancel orders if it hadn't been for what you've all done tonight and that would have been disastrous.' It had also been lovely getting to know her and we'd promised some nights out together in the New Year.

'That's what friends are for,' she said. 'Although you realise I'll need you to master sewing, knitting and crocheting so I can call on you next time I have a bear-making crisis, don't you?' She laughed at my shocked expression. 'Kidding! Honestly! Right, got to run. Take care.'

When she left the shop, I turned to Tara and gave her a grateful smile. 'I can't thank you enough for organising everyone tonight.'

She shook her head. 'It was Liam's idea and he'd have rounded them up himself if he'd known them. I reckon that man would walk over hot coals for you.'

I smiled. 'He's always been like that.'

Although Liam was clattering about in the kitchen, washing up, and unlikely to hear us, Tara lowered her voice. 'As for my Christmas wish? After tonight, I would confidently bet The Chocolate Pot that it's going to come true.'

Tears pricked my eyes. If only. 'What makes you so sure?'

'Everything. The looks, the touches, the affectionate stories.'

'You don't think that's just a really strong friendship?'

She shook her head. 'It's obvious that you have the strongest of bonds but it's not just friendship. There's chemistry and I'm not the only one who noticed. Sarah asked me if you were seeing each other and, when I said no, she said, "I bet they are by the end of the week". And, don't worry, I didn't tell her what you'd told me. I can keep secrets.'

'Thank you.' I thought about the secret she'd kept from me about her marriage to Garth. 'I trust you.'

She smiled. 'I know you're worried about your sister but that doesn't mean you can't be happy. Liam might only be home for a couple of weeks and then how long before you see him again? You'll kick yourself and probably start resenting her if you let the situation with Bethany get in the way of you two being together. Tell him or show him how you feel and don't even think about it being bad timing because, let's face it, how many things in life are perfect timing?'

Tears pricked my eyes again. She spoke with such wisdom and I felt so grateful to have her in my corner, recognising my turmoil and reassuring me it was okay to think about myself occasionally instead of being the ever-protective big sister. Tara had been there for me tonight and I'd be there for her whenever she was ready to talk about her failed marriage. She'd shared more with me this month than she'd shared in the past four years, making me wonder if she felt she could now trust me with whatever secrets lurked in her past, especially as I'd shared my biggest secret with her. Time would tell but I wouldn't push her. I'd just let her know I was there when – if – she felt ready.

'All washed up in there and...' Liam walked through the archway wiping his hands on a towel and stopped when he clocked Tara. 'Sorry. I thought you'd all gone.'

She smiled at him. 'I'm leaving now.' She turned to me. 'I've really enjoyed tonight. I might have skipped Pilates but I reckon rolling out that icing gave my arms just as good a workout.'

Hugging me, she whispered in my ear. 'Make that wish come true.'

'How are you holding up?' Liam asked after I'd locked the door behind Tara.

'Good, I think.' I yawned and stretched. 'I'm now ahead with work thanks to all of you. I can't believe you sorted that out for me. That was amazing.'

'Hey, I'm an engineer. It's in my DNA to fix things.' He grinned at me, then his voice softened. 'Seriously, though, I know how important this place is to you and how devastated you'd have been if you'd failed to deliver. I had to do something.'

'I'll be forever grateful to you.'

I made my way into the workshop and he followed.

'I don't think there's anything else we can do tonight,' I said. 'Do you want to stay here tonight or do you need to get back? Your parents probably think I've kidnapped you.'

'They understand and they're not home tonight anyway. They've gone to Newcastle to see a play with my Uncle Steve and Auntie Grace so I'll stay. Unless you've had enough of me.'

'I could never have enough of you.' Would he hear the real meaning in my words?

Liam held my gaze for a moment and that chemistry crackled again, just like Tara had said. I definitely wasn't imagining it but it was new, wasn't it? In all the years I'd been in love with Liam, I'd never felt even a hint that he might feel the same outside of that evening in The Old Theatre. Had something changed and he'd only just realised his feelings? Was I being more obvious and that had made him drop his guard? Or was it simply that the timing hadn't been right before, perhaps due to either of us being in relationships? So we'd both firmly pushed feelings aside and couldn't keep them hidden now that we were both single and he was at home for a decent amount of time.

It was on the tip of my tongue to add, 'As far as I'm concerned, you can stay forever.' I wasn't that brave, though. What I'd just said could be taken as a friendship thing if Liam wanted to take it that way and that was about as brave as I could be right now. It was taking all my emotional strength not to lose it again with worry about Bethany.

'You know what I could do with right now?' Liam said. 'An Irish coffee in front of a real log fire. Do you know anywhere round here that could accommodate that?'

I smiled. In our early twenties, we'd gone through a phase of always ending the evening with an Irish coffee, thinking that we were the height of sophistication.

'I think the little bistro upstairs might have what you're looking for,' I said.

* * *

Fifteen minutes later, the lounge fire was roaring, the fairy lights were casting a warm glow across the room and I'd lit a cranberry-scented Christmas candle.

'Ooh, that hits the mark,' Liam said taking a sip of his coffee. 'I can't believe you had some cream in your fridge.'

'Neither can I,' I admitted. 'I have no idea what made me add it to my online order. I must have had a psychic moment, knowing it would be needed.' I took a sip and smiled. 'Slightly stronger than we used to have, I think.'

'I think we both need it, Carls.' He relaxed back into the sofa. 'Do you remember that time when Bethany made us one of these with some out of date Bailey's and it all separated? That was disgusting.'

I laughed at the memory. 'Yes, and it took you about half the mug before you finally admitted it was gross.'

He nodded, smiling. 'I didn't want to look like a wimp and I didn't want to hurt her feelings.'

I took another sip. 'You know, I've never drunk Irish coffee with anyone but you. I think of it as our thing.'

'Same here,' Liam said. 'Sometimes even the simplest things have special memories and it's not the same trying to do it with someone else. I've never been camping with anyone else. That's our thing too. And do you remember when we stayed in those glamping pods on my birthday?'

'That was such a great evening,' I said, smiling at him. 'I remember how much...' I stopped mid-sentence and clapped my hand across my mouth.

'What is it? Are you okay?'

I put my mug down and stood up. 'I think I might know where Bethany is.'

'Really? Where?'

'Moor View Farm. The glamping pods. When you said it just now... I can't believe I didn't think of it before.'

We pulled on our boots, sprinted down the stairs and grabbed our coats.

'Wait! I need something.' I ran back up the stairs and grabbed a bag from behind the sofa. If Bethany was at Moor View Farm, she'd need convincing that she wasn't a failure and what I had in the bag might help.

Moor View Farm was perched on a hill outside Whitsborough Bay, overlooking the moors and Kittrig Forest. Before Liam had gone away to join the army, before Jasper, before Aimee and before Carly's Cupcakes, Liam had celebrated his twenty-fourth birthday at Moor View Farm after befriending the owner's son, Kev, who worked at the same company as him. He hadn't been planning on doing anything special for his birthday but Kev had told him that his parents had a last minute cancellation and, if he fancied celebrating in style with eight brand new glamping pods, a private bar with a fire pit and a hog roast, his parents could offer him a massive discount. It was too good an offer to turn down.

Due to the large capacity, Liam had extended the invitation to Bethany and her friends, aged fifteen and sixteen at the time, on the strict instructions that they'd be sent packing if they touched any alcohol. Bethany's friends were picked up by their parents at 11.00 p.m. but Bethany had special permission to stay overnight.

Liam and I had been impressed with the glamping pods but

Bethany had been completely smitten. They were each decorated with a different theme such as: country cottage, medieval, New England, seaside. Bethany and I were sharing and Liam insisted we had first pick. She chose the shabby chic pod, squealing with delight at the floral and gingham cushions, bunting and fairy lights.

'I could live here,' Bethany had said, lying down on the duvet, which was covered in floral campervans and tents. 'It's not just this pod that I love. It's how peaceful it is out here. When the sun set over the forest tonight, it was so beautiful, it made me want to cry.'

'I didn't know you were into the great outdoors,' I'd said.

'Neither did I, but this place is magical. I can't imagine ever feeling stressed or worried if I lived here.'

As far as I was aware, she'd never been back but she'd mentioned it before – years ago now – joking that she sometimes wished she lived away from Whitsborough Bay so that she could holiday at Moor View Farm. It had to be the place.

'Do you think we should have collected Joshua?' I asked Liam as I pulled onto the approach road towards Moor View Farm.

'I wondered that but what if we're wrong and she's not there? It's better that he doesn't know if it turns out to be a false alarm.'

I gripped the steering wheel as I turned into the glamping site. 'I'm so nervous. My heart's pounding.'

Liam placed his hand on my leg for a moment and gave me a reassuring squeeze but it made my heart race even faster – for a different reason. 'We'll soon know either way.'

The glamping pods weren't accessible by vehicles, which helped ensure a restful night for guests. As we pulled into the car park away from the pods, my heart thumped so fast that I felt sick. There was only one car at the far end.

'She's here!' I squealed as my headlights illuminated the yellow vehicle.

I pulled in beside Bethany's car and Liam grabbed my hand as we ran down the gravel pathway towards the glamping pods, our journey illuminated by white solar lights at feet level and above us.

The pods were stretched out before us and I pointed. 'Look! There's one with a light on.'

We crept towards the pod, not wanting to scare Bethany, although a knock on the door at 1.00 a.m. was bound to come as a shock. I lightly tapped on the wooden door.

'I can hear the TV,' Liam whispered. 'You'll have to knock louder.'

I knocked again. The sound from the TV stopped.

'Who's there?' came Bethany's voice.

'It's me. Carly,' I said. 'I've got Liam with me.'

The door opened outwards moments later and Bethany peeked round it. She squinted at us then pushed it wider. She looked rough. Her long hair hung in a dishevelled mess round her slumped shoulders and her pale face was completely devoid of emotion.

'How did you find me here?' She sounded so weary that I wanted to fling myself at her and hold her tightly. I had to keep telling myself that she'd needed space and I was going to need to do things slowly.

'I remembered how much you loved it here when we stayed on Liam's birthday,' I said.

She glanced at Liam and inclined her head towards him by way of a greeting, as though that was all she could muster the energy for. He gave her a gentle smile in return.

'We thought it was worth a look,' I continued. 'I know it's late and you're in your PJs but can we come in?'

Bethany shrugged but stepped back and let us pass.

'We've all been so worried about you,' I said when she closed the door, hoping I sounded concerned rather than angry with her.

Her shoulders slumped even further. 'I'm sorry.' She pulled her dressing gown tightly across her chest. 'I wasn't thinking.'

Shuffling awkwardly in the middle of the glamping pod, fiddling with the belt on her dressing gown, my sister looked so lost and vulnerable, exactly how she'd looked after she was stabbed. I couldn't hold back any longer and reached out to draw her into a hug. She was rigid at first, then seemed to relax. Moments later, the tears started to flow. Her hold tightened as she cried and I stroked her back and whispered soothing words.

When Bethany seemed to have got over the worst of it, I led her to the floral sofa and sat her down. Liam had already sat down on one of the painted dining chairs.

'Please talk to me, Bethany. Why did you leave like that?'

'I couldn't do it anymore.' She wiped her cheeks with the belt of her dressing gown and sniffed.

'Do what?'

'Any of it. I kept messing things up and I could feel this huge ball of panic inside me getting bigger and bigger. I needed to be where other people weren't so I could calm down and clear my head. This was the only place I could think of where I knew I'd be able to do that.'

'And are you feeling calmer?'

She nodded. 'The panic attacks have stopped.'

I grabbed her hand, my stomach churning. 'You've been having actual panic attacks?'

She nodded again. 'Two or three a day.'

'Bethany! Why didn't you say anything?'

She hung her head. 'I was ashamed.'

'No!' I cried, squeezing her hand tighter. 'Please don't feel that way. We could have helped you.'

She let go of my hand and folded her arms across her chest. 'And that's exactly why I couldn't tell you and why I'm ashamed.

You've all done so much for me already. You, Mum and Dad have picked me up after every failed job, every failed relationship and after what happened at Sandy Shores. They've skipped holidays to take time off work to look after me, they've kept a roof over my head and given me money and you've given me a job. And as for Joshua...' Her voice broke and the tears started flowing again. 'He gave me everything. What have I ever given any of you in return except stress and worry?'

'You've given us you.' I fought to keep my voice strong even though my heart was breaking at the thought of my little sister hiding panic attacks from the people who loved her because she was ashamed. 'The only reason we worry is because we love you and it's not your fault that life dealt you a few tough blows. When you love someone, it's not all about the good times. It's about helping them through the challenges too.'

She didn't say anything but she nodded so I was confident my words were sinking in. 'When did the panic attacks start?'

'After I tried to go back to Sandy Shores that second time.'

I closed my eyes for a moment, trying to push back the guilt and pain. Six months she'd suffered in silence. Six whole months. She wasn't the failure. We were!

Opening my eyes, I looked towards Liam. He gave me a subtle thumbs up and mouthed, 'You've got this.'

'What do you say to speaking to a doctor about the panic attacks?' I asked, gently pushing a clump of hair away from Bethany's face.

'I say that's probably a good idea.'

'Good. We'll get that sorted.' I looked over at Liam again and he nodded encouragingly. 'And... erm... what about Joshua?'

She finally looked up at me, her eyes red and puffy. 'What about him?'

'He's frantic with worry about you. He'd be here right now but we didn't tell him we were coming in case we were wrong and you weren't here. Do you still love him?'

She sighed as fresh tears trickled down her cheeks. 'I'm not good enough for him,' she whispered.

'That's not what I asked. I asked whether you still love him.'

'Of course I do, but he deserves—'

'To be happy,' I cut across her. 'And do you know what makes him happy? Being with you.'

She gave me a weak smile.

'Do you still want to marry him?' I asked.

'Yes!' she cried but her expression darkened. 'I can't put him through it. I attract disaster. I nearly died.'

I gathered her in a hug again, as much for my comfort as hers. 'But you didn't die. You were in the wrong place at the wrong time. That's all. If anything, what happened at Sandy Shores should prove to you how precious life is and how you've got to make the most of the time you've got because none of us know when our time is up. Don't forget how you met Joshua so you're not the only one who's had a brush with death.'

I released her and looked at her earnestly. 'You literally saved his life and now it's your chance to let him do what he can to help you get yours back on track. He wants you home. He still wants to marry you on Friday but he's happy to wait if you need more time. He just wants you back.'

'He needs to find someone he can be proud of, not someone who fails at everything.' I could hear the uncertainty in her tone and knew I was close to convincing her.

'That's rubbish, and you know it.' I took a deep breath and adopted a stern tone. 'Seriously, Bethany, you have to stop with this failure thing. I completely understand where the panic attacks have come from and we'll get you some help for that but I don't know how this failure thing started and you need to change the record.

You are *not* a failure. Here.' I lifted the card out of the bag I'd brought and thrust it into Bethany's hands.

'What's this?'

'You drawing my future without me realising. You even named the shop Carly's Cupcakes and never took credit.'

'That's because it was Mrs Armstrong's idea.'

'No. You suggested it first. You planted that seed of belief.'

Bethany flipped open the card and looked at her artwork, a shadow of a smile on her lips. Then she shrugged and handed it back to me. 'So I made a nice card when I was nineteen. You're the one who made the business happen. I nearly destroyed it.'

I shook my head. 'I might have had to give away the penguin cake and I'd be lying if I said there haven't been cupcake casualties but you've more than made up for that. I've been getting orders using a promo code I couldn't place and I spotted it on a box of fliers in the storeroom earlier. Half the fliers had gone. You've been handing them out, haven't you?'

'I spotted them when I was doing that fake stocktake and put some in my bag. I felt guilty for storming out last week so I dropped them round a few places.' She smiled for the first time. 'You've had some calls?'

'Loads. I've already taken bookings for next year, thanks to you, including a commission to supply Bay View Care Home with cakes every time one of their residents has a birthday. Do you know how many residents they have? Seventy-five!'

Bethany's eyes lit up. 'They really got in touch? The manager said she might be interested, but I thought she was just being friendly.'

'They really got in touch. *You* made that happen. You!'

Bethany shrugged dismissively but I could tell from a hint of colour returning to her cheeks that she was pretty pleased with herself. 'Well, I'd messed up so I wanted to try and put things right.'

'You succeeded. And I've been thinking about all the other things you've done for the shop like all the times you've upsold to customers and the marketing ideas you've given me, and I've realised I made a massive mistake in trying to turn you into a duplicate me. Cake decorating is *not* your talent but you have lots of other talents that I should be making more use of. I want you to retract your resignation, which I never formally accepted anyway, and I want you to become my assistant manager.'

'What?' Bethany's eyes widened with clear shock. 'Have you been sniffing your food colourings?'

'I'm serious. You'll be in charge of running the shop side, managing the marketing and promotions, and handling the social media.'

She released a snort of laughter. 'Social media? After penguin-gate? You must be kidding.'

'Penguin-gate wouldn't have happened if you'd known about my social media policy. It was a genuine mistake. Plus, there's something else I want you to do. You're an amazing artist and I'd forgotten how good you were until I found this card. I could use your artistic talents.'

'How?'

'Customers mainly come in with a picture of something they've found online that they want me to replicate. I won't copy someone else's design but it provides me with inspiration to produce something similar. But sometimes they come in with a vision and no picture. I'm no artist so I have to go for it and hope I've interpreted their vision right. My artistic assistant manager could design bespoke cakes for our customers and they get a cake and an original drawing. Pretty unique selling point for us.'

Bethany's eyes lit up and I had a momentary glimpse of the happy carefree woman I was used to seeing. 'You think I could do that? The drawing thing, I mean?'

'Definitely. And all the rest of it. What do you think?'

'What if I mess it up?'

'By doing what? You've already had successes when you haven't even been trying. If you're properly focusing on it, imagine what you could achieve. Don't say anything yet. Just think about it.'

She stood up and put another log into the burner. When she sat back down on the sofa, I handed her the card from Bear With Me.

'"A bear hug a day keeps the dark skies away",' she read. 'Cute picture.' She opened the card and her eyes filled with tears as she read the words that I'd written inside when I couldn't sleep the night she went missing:

*I know you think you screw things up and fail at every turn*
*I know you find that certain tasks are really hard to learn*
*I know you think you cost me cash and mess my business up*
*I know you worry all the time that you're not good enough*
*You call yourself a failure, and put yourself right down*
*It even made you run away; escape out of this town*

*I really wish you'd see yourself as the success you are*
*The way you speak to customers; you're such a shining star*
*Just look at how the sales reports increase for every week*
*And think of how you make me laugh till tears roll down my cheek*
*See how good a friend you are, so caring and so true*
*How good you are at drawing; I wish I were like you*

*I found this bear in 'Bear With Me'. He really made me smile*
*He's just like you and Christmas lights, all tangled up in style*
*You may sometimes be clumsy, but that's what makes you you*

*Please come back and work with me; without you I'm so blue*
*There's so much that you're good at, that's no word of a lie*
*Be my assistant manager. Go on, give it a try*

*Don't let those dark skies block your brightness*

*Hug a bear, hug your husband, and hug your sister*
   *All my love, Carly xxx*

'What bear?' The words were barely audible as she wiped the tears from her cheeks once more.

'This bear.' I removed Tangled from the bag and passed him to Bethany. 'Consider him an early Christmas present and a promotion gift. As soon as I saw him, I thought of you.'

Bethany stared at the bear, tears pooling in her eyes. 'He's gorgeous. I love him. Thank you.'

'Do you love him enough to accept my job offer?'

Bethany chewed on her bottom lip for a moment, still staring at the bear. She picked up the card and looked at the message again.

'You really think I can do this?'

'I don't just think you can do it; I *know* you can do it. The business needs you. I need you. Do we have a deal?'

She gave me a weak smile. 'I'll think about it.'

'That's better than a no so I'll take that for now. And will you stop putting yourself down?'

'I'll try.'

'And can we get you home to your fiancé?'

She nodded slowly.

'Good.' I stood up. 'Grab what you need and you can come back for the rest of your stuff in the morning.'

'Do you need me back at work tomorrow?'

'No. It's all covered. Spend some time with Joshua, get ready for your wedding, and return to me as my assistant manager after your honeymoon.'

As we walked back to the car, arm in arm, Bethany still in her nightwear, I felt lightheaded with relief. My sister was safe and well and the business was back on track. Nearly everything was resolved … except for the situation with Liam. Was I strong enough to try for the hat-trick tonight?

## 18

FIVE DAYS UNTIL CHRISTMAS

'Visitors for you,' Lana called from the shop side the following morning.

I put down my piping bag and headed into the shop, grinning at the sight of Bethany and Joshua with their arms round each other, looking relaxed and radiant.

'We wanted to stop by to say thank you for last night and for everything,' Bethany said.

Joshua stepped forward and hugged me. 'I can't thank you enough for bringing her back to me. I've been lost without her.'

'I know you have.' I squeezed him tightly, picturing the expression of sheer joy on his face when he'd opened the door of their home last night to the sight of Bethany getting out of my car. He'd run out in his bare feet, arms outstretched, clearly ecstatic to have her back.

'I also wanted to say yes to the job offer,' Bethany said, her voice full of doubt. 'If you're sure and it wasn't just a ploy to...' She tailed off as Joshua lightly nudged her in the ribs. She glanced at him and he nodded encouragingly. She smiled then cleared her throat and announced in a much louder, confident tone. 'Thank you for offering me the job of assistant manager. I would like to officially accept it and look forward to starting my new role in the New Year.'

'Welcome back to Carly's Cupcakes.' I gave her a tight squeeze and kissed her on the cheek. 'And welcome back to the real Bethany who believes in herself and doesn't put herself down.'

'We're going to have a putdown jar at home,' she said. 'And I think we might need one for here too. It's like a swear box only I have to put £1 in every time I call myself a failure.'

'Sounds like a great idea.'

'And I've got an appointment to see my doctor tomorrow.'

Joshua cuddled Bethany to his side once more. 'We think she might have post-traumatic stress disorder from the stabbing.'

I nodded. 'Liam thought that too.' He'd suggested it as soon as we'd driven away from Bethany's last night. He'd seen a lot of PTSD during his years in the army and had recognised it in her. 'I'm glad you've set the ball rolling to get some help.'

'One of my clients is a life coach,' Joshua said. 'She specialises in things like confidence building and assertiveness. We're going to set up some sessions with her for after the honeymoon, see if we can work out where the self-esteem issues have come from and take it from there.'

Bethany nodded. 'I'm feeling okay at the moment and I'm excited about the wedding and the new job, but I'm not naïve enough to think this has magically disappeared. Running away this week was a pretty extreme reaction and I need to make sure it doesn't happen again. I can't run away every time things get tough and you're right about me putting myself down. I've been doing it for years but it's got worse since the stabbing. I need to get control of it.'

'Whatever support you need from me, just say the word.'

'Thank you. We'd better let you get on but is Liam here?' she asked. 'We wanted to thank him too.'

'No. He's finally been allowed to escape and spend some time with his parents.'

Bethany handed me an envelope. 'In that case, can you give him this? I know it's really short notice but we'd both love it he could come to our wedding. With Paige dropping out, we happen to be a guest short.' She giggled. 'But tell him I'm not expecting him to wear her bridesmaid dress.'

I laughed too. 'Oh, I don't know. I think he'd look pretty good in it.'

'If it had been the one-shouldered one, I'd agree, but I'm not sure strapless is quite him.'

It warmed my heart to see Bethany smiling and I felt a pang of guilt again that I'd worked beside her for months and had been too busy to notice when the laughter had ceased until it became too late.

'I'm seeing Liam tonight,' I said. The amazing teamwork last night getting me ahead with my orders meant I could take an evening off and go out for that meal with him, a day later than planned. 'I'll give him this and I'm sure he'd love to come.'

The door opened and a couple of customers came in and headed towards the counter where Lana took their cupcake order.

'We'll head off,' Bethany said. 'We're meeting Mum and Dad for lunch and there's a lot to tell them.'

'They'll understand and they'll be supportive.'

She smiled. 'I know. They always are. I'm lucky to have such a great family. Thanks again for everything.'

I gave them both another hug then returned to the workshop, clutching Liam's wedding invitation, while Lana served some more customers. I released a shaky breath as I sat down at the table and gathered my thoughts. It was great to see Bethany and Joshua looking happy but the best part of their visit was knowing they were getting Bethany the help she so clearly needed. She'd hidden her PTSD and we'd all swept the self-esteem issues under the carpet, not realising they were part of a much deeper problem. There could have been disastrous consequences in doing that but I refused to dwell on those. It was out in the open now and I felt particularly pleased that the doctor's appointment was tomorrow. It would have been easy to put that off until after the honeymoon, especially when they likely had so much to do before Friday's wedding. She was on her way to getting professional help and we'd all be there for her with love and support and also some space. I'd definitely smothered her and our parents had too which had undoubtedly exacerbated the problems.

I stood in front of the full-length mirror on my bedroom wall that evening, twisting and turning. My usual work attire was jeans or leggings with a T-shirt or casual shirt – comfortable and practical for baking and decorating. Wearing a dress and heeled boots felt quite alien to me but I wanted to look my best so I'd dug out a classy burgundy dress which had been loitering in my wardrobe for a couple of years, begging for an occasion to be worn.

The door buzzer rang sending the butterflies in my stomach into a frenzy.

'I'll be right down,' I said into the intercom, before grabbing my bag and heading downstairs to put my coat on.

It wasn't a date but it felt like it. I'd texted Tara first thing to let her know Bethany was safe and then again on the afternoon to say I'd rearranged my meal with Liam. Minutes later, she'd turned up on the pretence of bringing hot chocolate for Lana and me but really to give me another pep talk about it being the perfect opportunity to tell Liam how I felt, especially now that Bethany was home.

I'd decided against going for the hat-trick last night. A conversation about my sister potentially suffering from PTSD wasn't a natural lead-in to a relationship conversation. Me releasing the most enormous yawn and saying to Liam, 'I am soooo tired. I can't wait to crawl into my bed and sleep now that I know she's safe,' hadn't exactly sent out a 'let's talk about us' message either. I'd felt drained by the time we arrived back at the flat, barely able to climb the stairs, never mind have a serious conversation about feelings and Liam's eyes were bloodshot with fatigue too. We'd clambered into bed with barely a word and had been out like lights.

'Wow! You look amazing,' Liam said, when I answered the door. 'I like the hair.' For the first time ever, I'd curled my hair using a wand that Bethany had given me last Christmas.

'Thank you. So do you.' He'd shaved and looked revitalised.

As we wandered down to the seafront, I told Liam about Joshua and Bethany's visit to the shop. 'They've given me a wedding invitation for you. Do you have any plans for Friday?'

'I do now. Are you on the top table or will I be able to sit next to you?'

'The top table is bride, groom and parents only so hopefully we'll be together. I'll throw a strop and refuse to be a bridesmaid if we're not.'

Liam laughed. 'I can't imagine you ever throwing a strop. It's not in your nature.'

'Oh, I don't know. You should see me with a rolling pin when one of my designs isn't going right. I once pummelled a pig to death. It wasn't pretty.'

'I hope we're still talking about icing here,' Liam said.

We arrived onto the seafront. Alternate red and green strings of lights lit the curve of South Bay and a twelve-foot tree next to the lifeboat station, covered in colourful lights, swayed in the wind.

'I've always loved it down here out of season,' I said, taking a moment to breathe it in. The arcades were still lit up so it looked seasidey and inviting, but it didn't have the crowds of tourists.

I closed my eyes for a moment as a gust of wind whipped my hair across my cheeks. When I opened them, Liam was gazing at me, an unreadable expression on his face.

'What's up?' I asked as the wind whipped my hair again.

Liam smiled, shook his head and reached forward and brushed a curl away from my face, making my stomach somersault. He opened his mouth as if to say something, then shook his head once more. 'Ready for food?'

Even though I'd barely eaten all day, I struggled with my meal. Tara's encouraging words swirled round my head but my stomach was in knots as I kept trying to psych myself up to saying something. *Liam, can we talk? Liam, there's something I've been meaning to say to you for ages. Liam, is there any chance we could be something more than friends?* Argh! I simply couldn't seem to find the right opening line. A couple of glasses of wine hadn't helped give me any Dutch courage.

The waiter brought us Irish coffees to finish and I smiled as I raised mine in toast. 'To nostalgia,' I said.

'To nostalgia,' Liam agreed.

We both took a sip, then fell silent. There was *never* silence between us. I desperately tried to think of something to say but all I could think of was those terrible conversation openers.

'It's a bit chilly out tonight,' I said, kicking myself that I'd resorted to a conversation about the weather of all things. What was wrong with me?

'It's that wind. I'd nearly forgotten what a vicious bite it has. It's a shame the snow's gone.'

'I know! I'm gutted that you missed most of it.'

Liam sipped on his drink again. 'Speaking of nostalgia and of snow, I loved that picture of you making a snow angel. With everything that happened with Bethany, I forgot to say. It took me right back to that day in Farmer Duggan's field.' He held my gaze and suddenly that spark between us ignited again.

'That was a special moment.' I gave him a tender smile. 'Until we got pelted with snowballs by the Biscuit Bunch and their Neanderthal mates.'

'The Biscuit Bunch.' Liam shook his head. 'Now there's an unpleasant blast from the past.'

'I was thinking about them the other day,' I said. 'Do you remember when we saw the Chief Biscuit in The Old Theatre and she started flirting with you?'

'Another special moment,' he said, his eyes twinkling as he smiled at me.

I cast my eyes down, my stomach sinking. Liam must have registered what he'd said because he swiftly back-tracked. 'Not special because the Chief Biscuit was flirting with me. God, no!' He pulled a face and did a dramatic shudder. 'I meant before that and after that. Just one of the many amazing times with you.'

It was the perfect moment to blurt it out but I couldn't find the words so I simply smiled.

Silence settled on us once more as I fiddled with my empty coffee glass.

'Do you fancy a walk along the seafront?' Liam asked. 'I know there's the wind chill but—'

I nodded. 'A walk would be lovely.'

While Liam settled the bill, refusing to go halves, I imagined every scenario from him taking me in his arms in the shadow of the lighthouse, declaring his undying love and kissing me passionately to him telling me he'd been trying to build up to letting me know he'd met someone else. I hated my imagination sometimes.

We set off along the seafront towards the harbour where the warm yellow beam from the lighthouse swept back and forth across the inky water. The wind carried a varied pitch of jangling sounds from the rigging on the moored sailing boats. I loved that sound. Like the squawk of gulls and the crash of waves, it made me think of home and, specifically, of Liam and the thousands of hours we must have spent on the seafront over the years.

The wind whipped my hair and I swiftly fastened the buttons on my coat.

'It's too cold, isn't it?' Liam said.

'No! Well, yes it *is* cold but not too cold for a walk. It must be a shock to your system after the heat of Afghanistan.'

'Just a bit, but I'd take this any day of the week.'

'I'm so glad you're back,' I said. 'I've missed you so much.'

'Same here.'

We continued in silence and I wondered whether to just blurt out, 'Liam, I love you and have done forever.' What was the worst that could happen? But that was the problem. I knew what the worst reaction could be. I opened my mouth several times, but I couldn't seem to eject the words. I thought about my question to the bears in Jemma's shop window: *Do you dare me to be brave and tell him how I feel?* I desperately wanted to be brave, but Bethany feared failure and it seemed that I feared rejection.

We made it to the harbour and rested against the Victorian metal railings. Dinky rowing boats, small motorboats, large yachts and a couple of pleasure cruisers dipped and soared on the choppy sea. White lights illuminated some of them and others bore colourful Christmas decorations. The sound of flapping sails mingled with the jangling noises and I breathed it all in.

'Do you want to know why I joined the army?' Liam asked after a while.

I frowned. He'd told me why when he broke the news. 'You said you wanted to travel the world.'

He gently nudged into me. 'And do you want to know the *real* reason?'

'I thought that was the *real* reason. Okay. Hit me with it. I'm intrigued.'

'I wanted to get out of Whitsborough Bay.'

My frown deepened. 'Why? I thought you loved it here.' I swept my arm across the harbour. 'Even when the Biscuit Bunch were at their worst, you always said that you couldn't imagine settling down anywhere else.'

Liam looked up towards the lighthouse then turned his gaze back to the boats. 'I still feel the same. This place is home and always will be.'

'Then why did you want to leave?'

'Wanted is probably the wrong choice of word. I probably should have said needed. I *needed* to get out of Whitsborough Bay.'

'Why?'

Liam turned to face me and took a deep breath. 'Because of you, Carls.'

'Me? Why? What had I done?' My stomach churned. This wasn't going how I'd imagined it in any of my scenarios. What was he building up to?

'You hadn't done anything. It was what I'd done that was the problem.'

I hardly dared ask. 'What had you done?' The nervous butterflies swooped and soared.

Liam took another deep breath. 'I'd made snow angels in Farmer Duggan's field with my best friend and, in the few minutes that we lay there, holding hands, before the Biscuit Bunch launched their attack, I realised I'd fallen in love with her. The thing was, I didn't know how to tell her. I kept telling myself I'd grow out of it and it was just an infatuation because we were outcasts together, but the years passed and I couldn't ignore that it was the real thing.'

I struggled to get the words out over the lump in my throat. 'Why didn't you say anything?'

'How could I? You only saw me as a friend as you so vehemently pointed out to the Chief Biscuit that time in The Old Theatre and afterwards to me when I asked if it would bother you if I called her. I figured that I could keep quiet and keep you in my life, or I could speak up and risk losing you. Both ideas were painful but the thought of losing you was worse.'

'You should have said something.'

Liam shook his head. 'You have no idea how many times I plucked up the courage, then chickened out. And it was fine ... until you got your first boyfriend. And any time you met someone after that, I knew he could turn out to be the one, and I realised I couldn't be there to watch it. I knew I'd missed my chance and I needed to get some distance and hopefully get over you.' He looked back at the harbour again. 'Sorry. That was a big information dump but I told myself that, if there was only one thing I did this Christmas, that had to be it.'

I felt like I was in a dream. I'd heard the words but I still wasn't 100 per cent sure I'd heard them correctly. 'How do you feel now?' I asked tentatively.

'Unsure as to whether I should have told you that.' He tightened his grip on the railings and I felt the uncertainty in every word – the fear of rejection, the worry of losing a friend.

I placed my hand over his. 'That's not what I mean. I mean how do you feel about me now?'

'You know that saying about absence making the heart grow fonder? It's true, I'm afraid. I may have physically moved away from you, but I never could emotionally. You're in here...' He pointed to his head, '... and in here.' He pointed to his heart. 'I don't think I have a single happy memory that isn't all about you.'

'Me neither.'

He looked down at my hand over his then into my eyes. 'You haven't run a mile. Yet.'

'And I'm not going to. For a start, have you seen the heels I'm wearing?'

Liam looked down and laughed. 'Good point.'

'And secondly, there's this...' I leaned forward and very gently kissed him, fireworks exploding inside me at the sensation of my lips against his.

'Erm... I... erm... what was that for?'

'You're not the only one who's been keeping a secret. I've lost count of how many occasions I've been looking at my best friend and wondering what it would feel like to kiss him, but not daring to do anything about it in case he didn't feel the same way as I felt about him.'

Liam's eyes widened. 'Are you saying what I think you're saying?'

'I think that the Christmas magic was alive that day we made snow angels and it's never left me either. I love you too, Liam. Always have. Always will.'

'You really mean that?' he whispered. 'Not just as a friend?'

'I really mean that. You'll always be my best friend but my feelings run way deeper than that.'

'So we've wasted all these years?'

I nodded. 'Which means we can't waste a minute longer.'

Our first proper kiss was everything that I'd dreamed of. I'd worried that it might seem strange kissing my best friend, but it actually felt like the most natural thing in the world as though we were two jigsaw pieces that had been designed to fit together and had finally been united. The icy wind blew off the North Sea and whipped my hair, my coat, and my dress, but I didn't feel the cold. All I felt was the warmth of Liam's touch.

## 19

## Bethany and Joshua's Wedding

'There's something different about you today.' Bethany sat down on our parents' bed and narrowed her eyes at me.

'I'm wearing a bridesmaid dress?' I suggested, pulling my skirt wide and giving Bethany a twirl.

She shook her head. 'That's not it.'

'The posh make-up and hair do?'

'Not it either. It's you. You're glowing.'

I blushed. I'd agreed with Liam that we wouldn't tell anyone about finally moving out of the friend zone as we didn't want to steal any of the limelight from Bethany and Joshua, but I couldn't disguise how incredible it felt to finally love and be loved in return after so many years living in the land of unrequited love. I'd been on cloud nine since Wednesday night and didn't think I'd ever come down. 'I'm excited about your wedding day, of course.'

Bethany stared at me for a moment longer, then bent over and started to pull on her stockings. 'That's not it either. If it wasn't for the fact that I know you've done nothing but work these past few weeks, I'd think you'd met someone.'

'You *are* funny.' Luckily she was preoccupied and couldn't see my giveaway expression.

There was a knock on the door and Leyla poked her head round it. 'We're all dressed and the flowers have just arrived. Do you need a hand?'

'She's still on her stockings,' I said. 'Too much talking. Not enough action.'

'It's your fault,' Bethany cried, starting on her second stocking. 'I'm trying to work out what's different about Carly today. Don't you think she looks different, Leyla?'

Leyla studied me for a moment. 'Yeah, there's something about you. A kind of glow.'

'Give over you two,' I said. 'I'm excited about being a bridesmaid at my baby sister's wedding. That's all.'

Bethany standing up ready for her dress took the attention away from me. Leyla helped me lift the dress over Bethany's head, careful not to mess up her hair or brush against her make-up. While Leyla fussed with the skirts, I fastened the bodice from behind.

Amanda and Robyn appeared in the doorway.

'Stunning,' Robyn said.

'Gorgeous,' Amanda agreed.

I couldn't speak. Tears filled my eyes and I simply nodded at Bethany who grinned.

\* \* \*

'Congratulations.' Liam kissed Bethany on the cheek while the photographer took photos of Joshua, his best man and the ushers outside the church.

'Thank you,' Bethany said. 'And thanks for coming at such short notice. I'm liking the suit, by the way. You scrub up pretty well.'

Liam grinned. 'I could say the same about you. Nice dress, although the teddy bear slippers and fluffy dressing gown from the other night were a good look too.'

Bethany giggled. 'You're such a liar.'

Liam turned his attention to me. 'You're looking lovely too,' he said, gently kissing me on the cheek. I closed my eyes as I inhaled his aftershave and couldn't help reaching for his hand.

'That's it!' Bethany squealed, causing several guests to look over. 'That's what's different about you. You're not just friends anymore, are you?'

I tried to feign innocence, but I couldn't hide it.

'Oh my God! I knew you were perfect for each other. Didn't I say the other week that I'd always expected you to get together?'

'Yes, you did, and you were right.'

Bethany began firing questions at us but the photographer needed us for some more group shots.

'I need details,' Bethany whispered as we stood together for a bride and chief bridesmaid photo. '*Full* details.'

'There are no *full* details to tell.'

Bethany winked at me. 'You're the chief bridesmaid at a wedding and Liam's looking hotter than I've ever seen him. Believe me, by the morning, there *will* be full details for you to share.'

My stomach fluttered at the thought. Liam had stayed over on Wednesday night, but we'd spent most of the evening talking about the past – how he felt when I got serious with Jasper, how I felt when he moved in with Aimee, when both the relationships ended and all the occasions when we'd come close to confessing but had bottled it. He admitted to telling me a white lie about why he'd split up with Aimee. At the time, he'd told me that she'd accused him of seeing someone else but it turned out her accusations had been about his relationship with me. She'd realised that Liam was in love with me and, no matter how much he insisted we were only friends, jealousy consumed her until it broke them apart. In return, I admitted that him moving in with Aimee was what had prompted me to broach the subject of moving in with Jasper, resulting in the end of that relationship.

We'd barely spent any time together yesterday. Work had called me downstairs early on and Liam had a family commitment on Thursday night, taking him away to Newcastle. We had tonight, though. I had a double room booked at Cresterley Lodge, the reception venue, and had been trying – and failing – not to think about spending the night there with Liam.

The next half an hour or so whizzed past in a blur of photos. Bethany had been worried that it might be too cold to get many pictures at the church but the wind had dropped, making the conditions just right.

'I think it's going to snow,' I said to Liam, looking up at the sky. 'It's getting that pink tinge again.'

He looked up too. 'There's no snow forecast but I agree with you. I'd be quite happy to spend the next few days snowed in at Cresterley Lodge with my favourite snow angel.' He gently kissed me, taking my breath away. 'I'll see you there.'

Cresterley Lodge was a thirty-minute drive from the church. Situated on a cliff top with the sea on one side and the North Yorkshire Moors on the other, it was a stunning venue. The wedding organiser there had already contacted Bethany to warn her that the snow from the past week hadn't gone due to them being on higher ground, although there was no problem with access as the roads were clear. Bethany had been thrilled at the news and had rushed out to buy sparkly pink wellies for herself and sparkly silver ones for the bridesmaids, determined that snow would feature in the photos.

A mini coach had been organised for the wedding party to follow the wedding car to the reception.

'It's snowing!' squealed one of the little bridesmaids, banging her hands against the coach window. I wiped the steamed-up window next to me and, sure enough, the heavens had opened again and released large flakes.

The gritters had been out so the roads to Cresterley Lodge remained clear, but the snow deepened the higher we climbed onto the moors. I gazed contentedly out of the window. The photos were going to look magical.

My phone rang with a FaceTime request from Bethany.

'It's snowing!' she squealed and immediately held the screen up to the wedding car window, as if I couldn't see the flakes for myself from the coach.

'I know. Just as well you bought those wellies.'

She turned the phone back to her face. 'I'm so excited. When we get there, can you get the wedding party to go straight inside? They'll have about twenty minutes to check in and freshen up if they want to, but I need them to meet in the main lobby at half twelve. We'll do some photos inside then the photographer will do some outside ones so please make sure nobody gets soggy in the snow before then.'

'Yes, boss,' I said, smiling at her. It was great to hear her sounding so organised and in control.

Travelling up the long approach drive to Cresterley Lodge, I felt like I was in a winter wonderland. Snow-laden conifers flanked the driveway, intermittently broken up by snow-capped stone sculptures. For the last few hundred metres, colourful lights hung between the trees before the drive widened out into a large courtyard. I stood up and issued Bethany's instructions as we pulled up in front of the entrance, then ushered everyone off the coach, grinning at the excitable squeals of the bridesmaids – and not just from the little ones.

There was no chance of me relaxing or checking in. I had wellies to distribute, Bethany's dress to hold while she went to the toilet, and some emergency re-pinning and hair-spraying for Robyn after she'd somehow managed to wrap her faux-fur stole round her head instead of her shoulders and knock her up-do out of shape.

As soon as the inside photos were finished, we stepped outside into the snow in our sparkly wellies. The photographer organised us for some formal photos, then encouraged us to play in the snow for some informal shots, as long as we promised not to throw any snowballs directly at the bride or groom's faces. I suspected those informal photos would turn out to be the best.

When the photographer said she was finished with everyone except the bride and groom, the rest of us gratefully retired indoors to warm up and dry off. Liam was by my side immediately with a glass of bubbly. He led me over to the roaring fire at one end of the bar and dusted flecks of snow off my stole.

'It looked like you had fun out there, Carls,' he said, then gently kissed me.

'People will see,' I whispered.

He shrugged. 'Bethany knows and she wasn't bothered. If she's fine with it, then the whole world can know.'

'This is true.' I put my arms round his neck and kissed him back.

'I checked the seating plan while you were outside and we *are* sitting next to each other.'

'That's a relief. I kept forgetting to ask Bethany.' I narrowed my eyes at him. 'Why do you look as though we're on a table with the flatulent auntie and the homophobic grandma?'

Liam glanced round the room then took my hand and led me out of the bar. 'I need to show you.'

We stopped outside the Great Hall where the seating plan stood on an A-frame next to an enormous Christmas tree.

'That's our table.' Liam pointed at the plan.

I skimmed across the names, then gasped. 'Elodie Ashton-Smith. No!' My eyes met Liam's. 'Do you think that's the Chief Biscuit?'

He grimaced. 'How common do you think the name Elodie Ashton is? I'm assuming the Smith bit is whoever she's married to, poor sod.'

I released a frustrated squeal. I'd hoped never to see her or any of the Biscuit Bunch ever again. 'What's she doing here?'

'You said Joshua has a big family so she's either part of it or she's married into it.'

I sighed. 'Looks like the meal's going to be fun. If she starts calling me Bear Trap or you Skindiana Bones, she'll be wearing her dinner. I take it you haven't spotted her?'

He shook his head. 'I'm not sure I'd recognise her if I had. I haven't seen her for over thirteen years. She could have changed her hair colour or put on weight or—'

'I hope she's bald and thirty stone,' I snapped.

Liam cuddled me against him and kissed my forehead. 'No you don't because it's not in your nature to be nasty to anyone. Despite what the Biscuit Bunch did to us, I know you'll chat politely to her during the meal and be your usual charming self.'

I released a little growl. 'I hate that about myself. Absolute pushover.'

'Well, I love it about you and I think of it as strength and class. Come on, let's get back to the bar.'

We'd barely made it back before it was time for me to join the receiving line while guests filed in for the wedding breakfast. I didn't see anyone who could possibly be Elodie, although I noticed a few guests bypass the line-up. Anyone who knew the venue would be aware of a second entrance to the Great Hall so she could have used that.

With aching cheeks from smiling so much, I headed inside to take my seat before the bride and groom were announced.

Liam squeezed my hand. The chair next to mine with the place card of Oliver Ashton-Smith was vacant, and so was Elodie's seat. He shrugged and whispered, 'No shows?'

'Ladies and gentlemen, would you please be upstanding to welcome your bride and groom, Mr and Mrs Fox.'

Bethany and Joshua took their seats to applause and cheers and, soon after, waiting staff appeared with starters and distributed them round the room. A tall, slim woman with long blonde hair and a dark-haired boy of about six, clutching a soft polar bear, slipped into the empty chairs.

'Sorry we're late,' she said. 'I had to take this one to the toilet. I'm Elodie and this is Ollie.' She looked round the table, smiling.

My heart thumped. It *was* the Chief Biscuit and, annoyingly, the years had been kind to her. Not bald or thirty stone, then. I took a deep breath. Best get the reunion over with.

'Hi, Elodie,' I said. She clearly hadn't recognised Liam or me as she'd looked round the table. 'It's been a long time. I think it was The Old Theatre when we were eighteen.'

Elodie's eyes widened. 'Bear Trap?'

I raised an eyebrow, my teeth grinding as I picked up my knife and fork to tuck into my starter.

'Sorry,' Elodie said. 'I can't believe I said that. I mean...' She frowned again, obviously struggling to remember my real name. She glanced down but my place card was hidden behind my water glass.

'It's Carly and this is Liam.'

'Oh my God! Hi, Liam. Sorry, Carly. As you say, it's been a long time and a lot has happened since then. I should *not* have said that.' She nodded her head towards Ollie and added, 'Ever.'

'That's okay.' It wasn't, but I didn't want to start a fight, particularly in front of her son.

Beside me, Liam buttered his bread roll as an awkward silence settled on our side of the table. The four guests on the other side seemed to know each other and were engrossed in conversation.

'You're a bridesmaid,' Elodie said, breaking the silence. 'How do you know the bride?'

'Bethany's my little sister.'

'Lucky you. I'd have loved a sister. I had an older brother who called me names, beat me up, and deliberately broke my stuff. He lives in Thailand now and that's still a bit close for my liking.'

'Mummy, please will you butter my bun?'

As I watched Elodie helping her son, I wondered about her brother. I'd read somewhere that bullies were often bullied themselves and found their own victims to get that control back. Had that happened to Elodie?

Buttering complete, Elodie looked back up at me and smiled. 'Sorry about that.'

'That's okay. So what's your connection to the bride or groom?'

'I'm Joshua's family. Sort of.' She took a deep breath. 'Here goes... Ollie's dad, Marcus, was Joshua's cousin and we were engaged. He was killed in a car crash three years ago so I suppose that would have made me a cousin-in-law if there's such a thing, although we never actually made it up the aisle because he died four months before the wedding.'

'Oh my goodness! Elodie, I'm so sorry.'

'Sorry, Elodie. That's tough,' Liam said.

Elodie shrugged and smiled at us both. 'Thanks. These things happen and life goes on, eh?' She smiled down at Ollie.

'How old was Ollie?' Liam asked.

'He'd only just turned three so he doesn't remember his daddy. He's six now and he's the spitting image of Marcus.' She pointed to her name card. 'I took Marcus's name and hyphenated Ollie's so we could be the same.'

She told us that her mum would pick Ollie up later and that she had a new 'friend' who'd be joining her for the evening, it was early days in their 'friendship', but it was going well so far.

'What about you two?' Elodie asked, giving us a cheeky wink. 'Still *just* friends?'

I blushed. 'We were until very recently.'

'About time too. Everyone could tell that you two were made for each other. Life's too short, you know. Far too short. Get married, have babies, and make the most of whatever time you have left. Hopefully it will be a very, very long time. Don't regret the years you weren't together, though. Make the most of the ones ahead of you instead.'

\* \* \*

After we'd finished our starters, I nipped to the ladies. When I emerged, Liam was waiting for me.

'I thought you might need a hug,' he said, arms open.

'I feel so guilty about Elodie,' I said, cuddling up against his chest.

'I thought you might.' He didn't need to ask why because he knew. For years, we'd fantasised about all the horrible things we hoped would happen to the Biscuit Bunch as payback for how they'd hurt us. 'It was just words and it had no impact on them. Elodie's fiancé died in an accident. It's one of those things. It's sad, but it happens, and we didn't cause it.'

'I know. I just feel so bad for her, to be on her own with her little boy. And that stuff she said about her brother picking on her when she was little. Do you think he made her the way she was?'

He shrugged. 'She knew what it was like having someone making her life hell and she could have made sure she never made anyone else feel like that. Instead, she chose to be one of the horrible kids. She chose to be a bully and inflict on others the same emotional hurt and physical pain that her brother inflicted on her. That was her decision.'

We returned to the table moments before the main course was served.

'Do you work?' Elodie asked us both when everyone had tucked in.

'I'm a mechanical engineer in the Army,' Liam said. 'I've been posted in Afghanistan recently.'

'My daddy was an engineer,' Ollie said, looking up. 'That's right, isn't it Mummy?'

Elodie smiled at him. 'That's right, sweetheart.' She looked up at Liam again. 'He was a structural engineer, specialising in wind farms. Are you off back to Afghanistan after Christmas?'

'I'm not sure yet.'

I caught Liam's eye and he winked. We hadn't discussed it. I remembered asking him on the phone how long he was on leave for and his response had been vague. He'd said it depended. What did it depend on? Did it depend on me? My stomach did a somersault at the possibility.

'What about you, Carly?' Elodie asked.

'I bake and decorate cupcakes and occasions cakes. Do you know Carly's Cupcakes on Castle Street? It's my business. I opened it four years gone October.'

'No! That's your shop? We love that shop, don't we Ollie?'

'Is that the one with the polar bear cake in the window?' he asked.

I smiled at him. 'Yes it is. I gather you like polar bears.' I nodded towards the soft toy on his lap.

'I love polar bears. This is Ice Cube.' He rubbed my arm with the toy's nose.

'He's gorgeous.'

'Marcus bought him on our last Christmas together,' Elodie said. 'Ollie doesn't go anywhere without him.' She paused to help cut up some of Ollie's food then looked up at me again. 'I can't believe you own that shop. We've had cupcakes from you before and we love them, and we've been to parties where they've had your cakes. You're so talented.'

'Thank you.'

'I mean it. I could never do anything like that. I'm so impressed.'

'What do you do?' Liam asked.

'I'm a receptionist at the hospital. It's okay. The hours are good for fitting round Ollie. To be honest, I didn't have many career choices. As you might remember, I mucked about at school so I didn't come out with many qualifications. Serves me right.'

'Are you still in touch with the Bis... the girls you were friendly with at school?' I asked. It struck me that I'd hated the name-calling yet Liam and I had been just as guilty.

'Not really, Elodie said. 'Scarlett James had a little girl when we were eighteen then a boy two years later around the time that Chelsea Webster announced that she was expecting too ... by Scarlett's boyfriend.'

'Ooh!'

'Yeah, I know. Not nice. Scarlett ditched the boyfriend and emigrated to New Zealand with her parents. We're Facebook friends but she never comes back to the UK so I haven't seen her in a decade. The boyfriend moved in with Chelsea then did the dirty on her with another one of the group, Liv Barker, which pretty much broke down the friendships. Two of the others moved out of the area and the rest of us drifted apart.' She shook her head. 'Funny, isn't it? There were eight of us and we were inseparable at school yet none of us are friends now. There were only the two of you and you're still together after all this time. I think you two definitely had it right. I used to see you wandering round town together or out on your bikes. You were always smiling or laughing and I used to envy you.'

Liam raised an eyebrow. 'Us? Seriously?'

'What you two had was genuine and what I had was superficial. It was all bitchy competitiveness although I never realised it at the time. Looking back, I don't think I was a very nice person at school, was I?' She laughed at our uncomfortable expressions. 'I think you've just answered that. I'm sorry for everything I said or did that might have hurt you. I won't try to make excuses for it, but I am genuinely sorry. We don't think much of bullies, do we, Ollie?'

'No, Mummy. Alfie Bedlow is a mean boy and I don't play with him.'

'He certainly is, sweetheart. Come on, Ollie, let's go to the toilets and get your face wiped. There's gravy everywhere.'

The waiting staff appeared to clear away the plates.

'Wow!' I said. 'The Chief Biscuit just apologised.'

Liam nodded. 'I feel sorry for her and that's something I never thought I'd say about her or any of her cronies.'

'I guess people change, especially when life throws bad things at them. Do you think Bethany could have been bullied at school? Do you think that's where the failure thing comes from? Maybe Paige was the bully. She was always putting the girls down.'

'It's possible,' Liam agreed. 'You'll have to mention it to her before she starts that life coaching thing. It could be a good starting point.'

'I'll do that.'

He topped up my wine. 'Have a drink, Carls, and let's put the past behind us and focus on our future. Together. As Elodie says, life's too short, and she certainly knows that.'

I nodded. 'Sensible plan, but there's one more thing that I need to ask you about the past. That night in The Old Theatre, when Elodie wrote her phone number on your hand, you wouldn't wash it off. Why?'

Liam groaned. 'I was hoping you'd forgotten about that. It was my pathetic attempt at making you jealous. You'd already made it clear to Elodie that we were only friends but I'd been sure that you were about to kiss me before she came over. I hoped that pretending I might be interested in her would make you jealous enough to throw yourself at me. Pathetic, eh?'

I smiled. 'Very pathetic, but also very sweet. And you were right, by the way. I had been about to kiss you before she came over, or at least I'd been hoping you'd kiss me and I certainly wouldn't have pulled away.'

He shook his head. 'All those wasted years.'

'Who just said let's put the past behind us and focus on our future together?'

'That might have been me.' He raised his glass and clinked it against mine. 'To outcasts together, united forever.'

I grinned. 'I like that. Outcasts together, united forever.'

## 20

The wedding breakfast was over, the speeches were complete, and guests had a couple of hours of free time before the evening entertainment started.

I'd been relieved to see Joshua's mum, Margaret, hugging Bethany during the desserts and coffees. I'd find out later what Margaret had said, but it looked as though she might be apologising. To my surprise, Margaret then asked if she could have a word with me too and apologised for any hurt and distress she'd caused me as a result of the way she'd treated Bethany. She even gave me a hug and said she'd pop in to see me in the New Year about a couple of occasion cakes she needed. It had to have taken guts to apologise like that. I felt reassured that, although there would probably still be challenges ahead, a line had been drawn in the sand and both sides were going to make a big effort going forwards. I knew from Joshua that he'd had a huge row with his parents the day after Bethany disappeared and I wondered if they'd realised how easily they could lose their son if they didn't make peace with Bethany.

Bethany had loved the bride and groom bears on her cake. I'd kept them secret and had asked the wedding organiser to place them on top of the cake before the receiving line was formed. They transformed the simple design and also provided her and Joshua with a permanent keepsake of an amazing day. Joshua said he adored the 'wee Scottish fella' and that the pair would be given pride of place in their lounge.

Mum fell into step beside Liam and me as we left the Great Hall, holding hands. 'Would I be right in thinking that you two finally have news for us?' she asked.

We stopped and I smiled at her. 'We're not just friends anymore.'

'I knew it! Your dad said I was imagining things and you were never going to get your acts together.' She hugged Liam. 'I couldn't be more delighted. You know we think the world of you.'

'Thank you.'

'It's about time too,' she said when she released him. 'We were beginning to think we'd have to bang your heads together.'

My eyes widened and Liam gasped.

'Mum!' I cried. 'You mean you've known all these years?'

'Of course we have. And your parents have too, Liam.'

'Seriously?' he asked.

'And you never said anything?' I added.

She laughed. 'It wasn't up to us to meddle. We knew you'd work it out for yourselves when the time was right. There was no way you weren't going to end up together. Wait till I tell your dad I was right. He'll be gutted. Not that you're together, of course. He'll love that. But he'll be gutted that he lost the bet and I get to choose the next five Netflix films. I feel a serious dose of romcoms coming on. See you both later.' With another laugh, she headed in the direction of the bar.

Liam and I both exchanged astonished looks.

'I was *not* expecting that,' I said.

'Me neither.' He took my hand again and we left the Great Hall.

'That's both sets of parents, your sister and the Chief Biscuit. Seems everyone knew we should be together except us.'

'They probably *should* have banged our heads together,' I said. 'Could have saved a lot of angst.'

'Have you got those sparkly wellies handy?' he asked.

'They're still by the fire in the lobby. Why?'

'I'll go to the room and grab our coats. We're going outside but I promise it won't be for long.'

Five minutes later, we stepped out of the hotel and made our way down the freshly-salted stone steps. The snow had stopped falling around mid-afternoon and darkness had followed shortly afterwards.

Ahead of us, the fresh untouched snow glistened like a carpet of diamonds. I lifted my skirts above my boots and relished the satisfying first-footing crunch in the deeper snow. Liam did the same but winced as the snow slipped down the side of his shoes.

'I didn't think that one through,' he said. 'I don't suppose any of the bridesmaids are a size twelve?'

I laughed. 'Not quite. I think seven was the biggest.'

Liam took my hand and led me along the side of the building towards an open space, which was bathed in warm light from the hotel's windows. Covered in snow, I couldn't work out what the space was, but benches at the far side suggested probably a garden.

'Where are we going?' I asked.

'You'll see.'

We trudged across the snow and past the benches, then down a slight incline.

'We're here.' Liam pointed towards the right.

I followed his finger and smiled. There was a wooden fence with a stile over it and a sloping field behind it. 'Just like Farmer Duggan's field,' I said.

Liam sprinted – or tried to – towards the stile calling, 'Last one to the top buys the drinks all night.'

Watching him slip and slide in his best shoes, which certainly weren't designed for the wintery conditions, I hoisted my skirts up and raced after him. I beat him to the stile although I suspected he'd deliberately slowed down to let me.

Dropping to the other side, we grinned at each other then raced in opposite directions across the bottom of the field, up the sides and across the top. When we met in the middle, cheeks aglow and hearts racing, Liam kissed me quickly then grabbed my hand as we ran down the middle of the field, dropping to the ground to make snow angels.

'That was so much more fun than doing it on my own in the middle of Castle Street,' I said the moment I had enough breath to speak. 'Twice.'

'I still can't believe you did that. I wish I'd been there to see it.'

He held my outstretched hand and we gazed up at the starry sky, chests heaving as we gulped in the cold night air.

Liam turned his head towards mine and smiled at me. 'Sixteen years ago, almost to the day, we lay in Farmer Duggan's field doing this. I held your hand just like this and all I could think about was what it would be like to kiss you and how you might react if I told you that I wanted you as more than a friend.'

I smiled at him. 'Do you remember having a conversation in the field about what we really wanted? You said that you knew what your heart's desire was and you wanted to know mine. Was I yours?'

'You were. And now I finally have my wish.'

'I suppose the best things come to those who wait.'

'You're so right, Carls. Over the years, I used to think that not making a move that day was the biggest mistake of my life and something I'd always regret, but now I'm not so sure. In Afghanistan, the lads and I would sometimes talk about mistakes we'd made, regrets we had, things we wanted to change when we got home... assuming we got home, that was.... but what Elodie said earlier made me think. She's right. I don't want *any* time spent with you to be something I regret. I don't want to think of *any* aspect of our relationship as being a mistake. Even though we weren't a couple, I wouldn't trade a single moment of it because every moment together made us who we are today.' He gently squeezed my hand. 'What I prefer to think is that the timing wasn't right for us back then – like your mum said – and that life wanted us to experience a few things before it finally brought us together.'

'You do think the timing's right now, though?' I asked. 'This isn't your way of telling me that you really do want to run off with the Chief Biscuit?'

Liam's expression turned very solemn and, for a brief moment, my stomach sank.

'It's an interesting proposition,' he said. 'But why would I want biscuits when I can have cake?'

I grabbed a handful of snow with my free hand and threw it at him. 'You had me worried for a minute.'

'Sorry. I've been dying to use that line for ages.' Liam shifted position. 'I'm getting wet. This seemed like a good idea at the time. Fancy standing up?'

'Yes, please.'

He pulled me to my feet and kept hold of both of my hands. 'I may not have any regrets but I have learned lessons and one of those is about being completely honest. You'd asked me when I was going back to Afghanistan and I said it depended.'

'Yes. Vague or what?'

'I know, but when I said it on the phone, I had to be vague because the answer depended on how you reacted when I told you that I love you. If you'd wanted things to go on as before, then I could have retracted my notice and returned to Afghanistan.'

My heart raced. 'You've served notice? There's an option not to go back?'

Liam nodded. 'I hated being back here for such a short time in February so I put my notice in as soon as I returned. I've served my time, learned loads, got to the rank I wanted, but it's not for me anymore. I need to serve a few more months, but I can definitely stay in the UK until I'm fully discharged, if that's okay with you.'

I bounced up and down excitedly. 'Oh my goodness, Liam! That's brilliant news. And here was me thinking I'd already got my Christmas wish when you told me you loved me. What will you do when you're discharged?'

'I got in touch with my old boss and he said there's a job with my name on it anytime I'm ready to return. All I need is somewhere to live.'

I smiled as I stepped closer to him. 'What sort of place did you have in mind?'

'Well, my dream property would be a cosy flat in the town centre. I'm a sucker for an open fire, period features, fairy lights and candles on all year round, plus a well-stocked fridge including cream to make Irish coffees. And, ideally, it would be above a cake shop. I don't suppose you know anywhere that might fit that description, do you?'

'Hmm. Above a cake shop, you say? There can't be many of those around.'

'I'm a bit stumped, Carls. I can only think of one.'

'Me too. So how soon can you move in?'

Liam put his arms round my waist as I snaked mine round his neck.

'You mean it?' he asked.

'I mean it. As Elodie said, life's too short.'

'In that case, is Sunday too soon?'

'Sunday's perfect.'

He bent down and kissed me. My breathing quickened as he pulled me closer and intensified this kiss with a passion I'd never dreamed existed.

'And you can kiss me like that every day,' I said when we broke apart.

Liam smiled. 'Your wish is my command.'

He took my hand and we trudged through the snow towards the fence.

'I wished for Santa to deliver you to me on Christmas Eve,' I said, 'so, if you move in on Sunday, I'll be getting my wish.' I thought about Tara and how it had been her Christmas wish for me to get together with Liam. We'd had the briefest of FaceTime conversations and she'd squealed when I told her we'd finally got our acts together. The Chocolate Pot was too busy to talk for long but I'd promised her I'd catch up with her after work tomorrow to show her some wedding photos and give her the full details.

'I've got one condition,' Liam said as he clambered over the stile.

'What's that?'

'If I'm your Christmas wish, please can I arrive through the front door instead of in a sack down the chimney?'

I laughed as he helped me over the stile. 'I'll have a word with the man in red and see what we can arrange.'

As I jumped down into the snow, Liam cupped my face in his hands and gently kissed me, making my heart race once more. 'I'm not rushing you into this, am I?'

'I've waited for this moment for the best part of two decades. I'm more than happy to take things at a pace. Outcasts living together, forever.'

I placed my arms round his neck and pulled him close to me, kissing him gently at first and then with more longing, just like he'd done in the field. I wanted him to be sure that everything he felt, I felt too, just as deeply. He held me tightly, as though he never wanted to let me go, and I never wanted him to either. I was finally where I belonged.

I broke away and smiled. 'Stunning as our surroundings are, I'm shaking, you're shaking, and I can't feel my feet. There's still loads of time before the evening do. What do you say to us getting out of these wet clothes and warming up? Or should I say, warming each other up?'

'I'd say race you back to the hotel.' With a whoop, Liam ran towards the hotel, skidding in the snow.

I raced after him. The snow might have chilled my body but my heart was on fire. Liam was right – it hadn't been our time back then but it was now and I intended to grab every single moment of it, just like Elodie said.

There were still three sleeps till Christmas Day but what a Christmas it was shaping up to be. My sister was married, my business was thriving, I had some amazing friends who'd saved my business from hitting a crisis and my very best friend loved me as much as I loved him. And he was moving in with me. Christmas at Carly's Cupcakes had been everything I'd ever dreamed off, and a whole lot more. I couldn't be more excited about Liam and I facing the future, outcasts united, together forever.

# ACKNOWLEDGMENTS

I hope you've enjoyed *Christmas at Carly's Cupcakes,* especially as it was a book I never planned to write. Carly wasn't a character in my head and the shop didn't exist until I wrote my very first Christmas release, *Charlee and the Chocolate Shop* where I very briefly mentioned a shop called Carly's Cupcakes. Suddenly a story popped into my head about the owner and it showed no signs of disappearing so, of course, I had to tell Carly's tale.

This story has not changed title but it has been refreshed and re-edited under the expertise of my amazing publishers, Boldwood Books. One of the major changes is that it was originally written in the third person. I enjoyed doing this and it was a good experience in experimenting with my writing style but it has now been re-written in the first person and I think it's much better for it. I've added in a few new scenes and a bit more detail around some of the key relationships that Carly has with her sister, Liam and Tara which I hope anyone revisiting this refreshed version has enjoyed.

My thanks therefore start with Boldwood Books who, at the time that this book is released, will have published two brand new titles from me and five books from my back-catalogue including this one. My editor, Nia Beynon, is such a joy to work with. Her edits are so valuable in tightening the story and drawing out even more emotion from each scene. Thank you to the brilliant proof-reading work of Sue Lamprell and the gorgeous cover designed by Debbie Clement which depicts the moment where Carly steps out of her shop into a deserted Castle Street early one December morning to a covering of snow. She stands in the street breathing it in, eyes closed, arms outstretched, then runs up and down making those first footprints. It's absolutely perfect.

Writing a book in which cakes appear in pretty much every chapter is not an easy task for a cake-lover like me. Talk about bringing on cravings! Apologies if I've made you very hungry. I always wanted to learn how to decorate cakes. For my daughter's fifth birthday, I had a go at decorating her cake with the face of Minnie Mouse. Let's not say any more about that terrifying attempt and the black icing stains on everyone's teeth! A few years later, I attempted to make a Rapunzel cake, inspired by the wonderful Disney film, *Tangled*. Let's not go there either! Suffice to say, I don't have the natural talent or patience that my heroine, Carly, has when it comes to cake-decorating – I'm more like Bethany – but I do have a good understanding of the process. Several years ago, I was a business coach for a short while and a couple of my clients were setting themselves up as cake-decorators, although I had no idea at the time that the insights I gained from them would find their way into one of my books. My good friend and beta reader, Susan, is exceptionally talented at cake-decorating. So is my cousin, Lisa, and another good friend, Jackie. I've always been in awe of the creations they share on social media so thanks to all three for their inspiration.

Continuing with the thanks, I need to mention my amazing husband, Mark, and our daughter, Ashleigh. They know how happy I am when I'm immersed in my imaginary world and they never complain. Thankfully, Ashleigh is often locked in her own imaginary world too, writing her own stories, and Mark is capturing the real world in an imaginative way with his camera. He's exceptionally talented as you can see if you visit his website www.markheslingtonphotography.com where you'll find many stunning images of the North Yorkshire Coast where all my books are set.

For the original version of this book, I owe a big slab of cake to my team of beta readers. Jo Bartlett and Sharon Booth are extremely talented authors whose work I can't recommend enough (and they also have Christmas books out). At the time, they both had day jobs and their own writing projects yet they found time to read my work and help knock it into shape with a few incredibly helpful and insightful observations. My mum, Joyce Williams, plus my close friends, Susan Hockley and Liz Berry, were also invaluable in helping smooth out the edges. They spotted typos, questioned gaps, and flagged up moments when I'd gone far too Northern and they didn't know what I was wittering on about!

Thank you also to book blogger Joanne Baird. She's Scottish and kindly took a look at Joshua's speeches to make sure they were authentic. I really appreciated her tweaks.

If you've enjoyed *Christmas at Carly's Cupcakes,* we have a treat for you because *Starry Skies Over The Chocolate Pot Café* takes you back to Castle Street. It's Christmas Eve in The Chocolate Pot and Tara is putting on a brave face. The plot for *Starry Skies Over The Chocolate Pot Café* was another occasion when a fully-formed story suddenly popped into my head. Tara had been mentioned in previous books and I had a vague sense of her as a character but, when she unexpectedly revealed to Carly that she'd been married before, I knew I had another story to tell and *Starry Skies Over The Chocolate Pot Café* tells Tara's tale.

My final thanks go to you, my readers or listeners. If you've loved *Christmas at Carly's Cupcakes,* it would be really amazing and helpful if you could leave a review. Reviews make a massive difference to an author and I read all of mine. It's amazing to read really long ones, but you don't have to write much. A sentence is fine and even a positive rating if you don't feel comfortable writing a review.

Happy Christmas if you're reading this in the festive season, or Happy Easter/Happy summer if you're reading it at another point in the year. After all, a Christmas book doesn't have to just be for Christmas! I personally have fairy lights on at home all year round and, if I could get away with it, the tree would stay up too!

Big hugs

Jessica xx

# MORE FROM JESSICA REDLAND

We hope you enjoyed reading *Christmas at Carly's Cupcake*. If you did, please leave a review.

If you'd like to gift a copy, this book is also available as an ebook, digital audio download and audiobook CD.

Sign up to Jessica Redland's mailing list for news, competitions and updates on future books.

http://bit.ly/JessicaRedlandNewsletter

# ABOUT THE AUTHOR

**Jessica Redland** is the author of nine novels which are all set around the fictional location of Whitsborough Bay. Inspired by her hometown of Scarborough she writes uplifting women's fiction which has garnered many devoted fans.

Visit Jessica's website: https://www.jessicaredland.com/

Follow Jessica on social media:

 facebook.com/JessicaRedlandWriter

twitter.com/JessicaRedland

 instagram.com/JessicaRedlandWriter

bookbub.com/authors/jessica-redland